Holiday Brew Copyright © 2020 by Tansy Rayner Roberts

Cover art © 2020 Teresa Conner of Wolfsparrow Covers

"Halloween is Not A Verb" originally published on the Sheep Might Fly podcast ©2018

"Kissing Basilisks" originally published on the Sheep Might Fly podcast ©2020

ISBN: 978-0-6487639-1-8 (ebook)

ISBN: 978-0-6487639-2-5 (print)

🌸 Created with Vellum

HOLIDAY BREW

TANSY RAYNER ROBERTS

CONTENTS

HALLOWEEN IS NOT A VERB

PART ONE
TO HALLOWEEN OR NOT TO HALLOWEEN

PART TWO
HALLOWEENING

PART THREE
EPILOGUES ARE FOR WITCHES

SOLSTICE ON THE ROCKS

KISSING BASILISKS

HALLOWEEN IS NOT
A VERB

PART ONE

TO HALLOWEEN OR NOT TO HALLOWEEN

CHAPTER ONE
MISTAKES ARE MADE

VIOLA VALE HAD MADE a crucial error.

As a postgrad student, it wasn't unusual to be asked to run a tutorial group for first years. When her department asked her to volunteer, she signed right up. That was perfectly reasonable. It didn't even count as a bad life choice.

When she realised she had actually been handed a third year Advanced Course, that was when she should have said no. Teaching students her own age was bound to lead to trouble, and she knew it even as she ummed and erred.

But, as Professor M said blithely, who would be better qualified to take seminars on The Magical Application of Ancient Myth?

(Apart from Professor M herself, a lowkey genius and qualified expert in the field, who clearly had her own reasons for not wanting to run this class)

Yes, it was relevant to her thesis, and yes Viola could talk through the course content in her sleep.

So yes, she said yes.

Big mistake.

Third year advanced students meant Jules Nightshade and Sage McClaren, who had both independently decided to take this class despite it not being remotely relevant for either of their majors. The bastards.

Both men were brilliant, with abilities and intelligence far beyond their peers. Both were being fast-tracked for postgraduate work themselves, once they graduated later this year, though Jules had yet to commit to that; he had a lot of job offers.

Both men technically counted as friends, she supposed, though she went back and forth as to whether Sage counted as a mate now, or a frenemy one stolen band t-shirt away from being her nemesis. Jules had been Viola's ride-or-die BFF for most of her life; there was no escaping him now.

Both men were arseholes.

That wasn't even the worst part.

The worst part was, they still wanted to bang each other. This class gave her a front row seat for all the sexual tension, passive aggressive flirting, academic one-upmanship, and the magical equivalent of shaking tail feathers.

Right now, Sage and Jules were having the most offensively intense discussion about the Icarus myth from across the circle of chairs, apparently forgetting there was anyone else in the room.

The other students in the tutorial watched the two of them with a fascination that bordered on the perverse, some of them discreetly taking notes on Sage and Jules' increasingly outlandish theories. At least Viola was here to witness this, and would know what was up if the mid-semester essays all repeated the obnoxious proposal that the source of beeswax for Icarus' wings was in any way significant to the mythic narrative.

One student had a laptop balanced precariously across her thighs, typing madly. Viola was pretty sure she was writing fanfic.

Sage was red in the face. This often happened when he was anywhere near Jules. Jules himself had gone all cold and sarcastic. Frost crackled across his eyebrows.

The student's laptop made a small fritzing sound as the magic tensions in the room — from Sage, probably, though Jules wasn't helping — reached their zenith.

"Okay, we're stopping there," Viola said briskly. "You have to decide on your final practical project by next week, including group selection, or I'll pick a topic and a partner for you. I need an abstract covering the myth you intend to explore, and the relevant spellwork you'll be engaging in. Also an ethics statement if that spellwork involves living creatures — which yes, does include human subjects. We'll use next week's tutorial to cover Minoan symbolism, so read the last three chapters of *The Circead*." She pointed a finger at Sage. "You need to go drink a cup of coffee right the hell now."

"Sorry," he said with that wide, horrendously charming grin of his. He gave Jules a restrained bro nod which wasn't fooling anyone, and hurried out of the room.

Jules leaned back in his chair like he had nowhere else to be.

"You," Viola said impatiently, after the last of the students filed out. "Seriously, Jules?"

"Seriously what?"

"I thought—" and she checked herself briefly, because her department was relaxed about some things, but she should probably be careful what she might be overheard saying to a student. "I thought he was out of your system," she said finally, in a mutter.

"I have no idea what you're talking about, Vale," said Jules, entirely innocent.

"You're buying lunch," she grumbled.

CHAPTER TWO
SOMETHING'S COOKING

R0ckg0dde$$ has created this mirrorchat

Twinsies: no

R0ckg0dde$$: bats eyelashes

Twinsies: Change my name RN or I am out of this chat.

R0ckg0dde$$: you are literally the last person in the world who uses full stops in chat

R0ckg0dde$$: FINE

Twinsies is now: Hebe So Boring

Hebe So Boring: I hate you. Why even.

R0ckg0dde$$: the mums wanna know are we gonna Halloween this year

R0ckg0dde$$: ???

Hebe So Boring: I was waiting for the rest of the sentence to show up. But punctuation will do, I suppose.

R0ckg0dde$$: I laugh in the face of punctuation

R0ckg0dde$$: I used to laugh in the face of spelling but now mirrors have autocorrect wtf

Hebe So Boring: Don't you have a class right now?

R0ckg0dde$$: the mums wanna know are we hallowwwweeeeening?

Hebe So Boring: halloween is NOT a verb

R0ckg0dde$$: sure it is. To Halloween. Shall we Halloween? Baby, Halloween me so hard...

Hebe So Boring: is this conversation still about our Mums?

———

HEBE WAS STILL STARING at her phone when a hand lunged over her shoulder and smacked it out of her hand. "Holly!" she protested.

"Sorry not sorry," said her twin sister, swinging around her other side and making a try for Hebe's toasted panini. "Ow, hot, hot," she added, and dropped the sandwich back on the plate.

"You're a monster," said Hebe, pulling her tray protectively towards herself. "Get your own food."

"Broke till Friday. Gotta sing for my supper. Feed me." Holly made a sad emoji face, managing somehow to look both ironic and genuinely hungry.

"You're the worst," said Hebe. She grudgingly poked her sandwich halves further apart. "Wait until it cools down. What's with the Halloween thing?"

"It's October," said Holly, eyeing the sandwich as if it was about to make a leap for freedom.

"I know that. But Halloween is weeks away. You never plan ahead. Last year, Summer Solstice took you by surprise. Summer Solstice, Holly. The decorations were up in the shops for months ahead of time, our uni shuts down weeks before, and you were all: *hey why are there no students in this bar*?"

"I was distracted and broken-hearted."

Hebe blinked. "You were broken-hearted last Summer Solstice?"

"I don't know, probably." Holly jabbed a finger tip at the sandwich to see if it was cool enough to massacre yet. "I don't know why you're so suspicious."

"I'm not suspicious… I wasn't suspicious until you started throwing around words like *suspicious*."

"I'm being a good daughter and planning our social commitments thoughtfully," said Holly, eyes widening. "Halloweening in the city, with our friends… Halloweening in the country with our beloved family. Tricky choice. Gotta make the right decision."

"You're up to something," Hebe decided, and took a bite of her sandwich. It was still too hot to eat but if she didn't get in now, she'd lose the whole thing.

Holly had practically eaten her own half in three bites.

Sage landed at their table with a thump, his food tray laden with more cheeseburgers than a single person should eat, even one with the muscle mass of Those Arms. A wave of thaumaturgical heat came with him, like he had dragged a tropical weather front into the canteen.

"How was your class?" Hebe asked him, which was a simpler, less confrontational way of saying, *How's that class you took to mess with the tutor because she stole your favourite t-shirt, and also to flirt with the one boy in this university you really shouldn't be flirting with?*

Sage looked smugger than should be possible while chewing half a burger. "Inspiring. Challenging. Highly educational."

Smoke started to emanate from the burger he held.

"And you haven't had enough coffee today," Hebe sighed, passing him her untouched latte.

"What makes you — ow, shit!" The burger burst into flames. Sage dropped it, slapped the flames out with one cupped hand, and took a deep swallow of the latte. "Oops."

His magic settled in the air around them; Hebe no longer felt like she was about to burst into flames herself.

"If you keep letting your magic flare up around Jules Nightshade, you're gonna need a caffeine implant," said Holly. She bit into a cheeseburger.

Sage looked at her closely, and then at his plate. "Did you steal that from my plate?"

"I liberated it from the patriarchy."

"Hebe, Holly is misusing that one gender studies class she took to impress a hot professor," Sage whined.

"That's the most productive use I've seen her find for *any* of her classes," said Hebe.

Holly grumped. "You pick a year's classes at random *one time…*"

"Hey, I am not the patriarchy," added Sage, belatedly offended.

Hebe and Holly both tilted their heads at him.

"I mean," said Hebe. "You kind of are."

"Butternut pumpkins," said Holly.

Sage blinked. "Is that your safe-word?"

"I'm giving you this burger back because you're clearly mad with starvation," said Holly, placing the half she had not eaten on his plate, without taking her eyes off her phone. "The Mums need to know how many butternut pumpkins to put on the shopping list, so they need to know how many people are Halloweening with us."

"The answer is zero, zero butternut pumpkins," said Hebe with a sigh. "It's not even the season for root vegetables, it's spring."

"A pumpkin's not a root vegetable, it's a berry," said Sage. "Well, more of a melon. Definitely a fruit."

Hebe blinked. "That is… new information."

"Tis the season for the conversation about how pumpkins are out of season in Australia but whatever," said Holly. "You, Sage. To Halloween or not to Halloween?"

"Am I invited?" he asked.

"No one's invited," said Hebe at the same time that Holly said:

"Everyone's invited!"

"Okay," said Sage. "It is a while since I've tasted Agatha's butternut pumpkin surprise. I'm feeling nostalgic."

"I'll think about it," said Hebe, giving her sister a Look. "I have a lot of work to do."

"Fine, you think about it," said Holly. "But you'd better think up a good excuse if you're not gonna Halloween with the rest of us. Once the mums start texting you instead of me, you know they mean business."

CHAPTER THREE

FROM THE JOURNAL OF MISS JUNIPER CRESSWELL, LADY CELLIST AND POETESS-IN-TRAINING.

FERDINAND CHAUVELIN IS MANY THINGS: a fine young gentleman with reasonable manners, a handsome devil, and a purchaser of unnecessarily extravagant silk shirts.

He was not, however, born under a rhyming planet.

Mere hours ago, I consoled him as he lamented his inability to master the course we are taking together at the College of the Unreal: Victorian Poetry Methods in the 21st Century.

"I'm not used to being bad at things," he moaned, flapping his D-grade paper at me and then draping himself decoratively over a library chair in order to properly mope.

(The full nature of his decorative qualities were largely lost on me, thanks to my Sapphic leanings, but I recognised the aesthetic he was going for.)

"It's good for you, I expect," remarked Holly, who had no good reason to be in this part of the library and yet, somehow, had appeared. She at least, as a card-carrying bisexual, could provide a more appreciative audience for Ferd's dramatic poses, were he not in love with her sister. "Trying something that doesn't come easy. A challenge is good for the soul."

Still splayed out over his chair, Ferdinand's eyes narrowed. "I'm sorry, did you just say to my brown face that I haven't had enough challenges in my life?"

Holly batted her eyelashes at him. "Yeah, nice try, but my

white guilt didn't make you sign up for a Victorian poetry course, basilisk boy. That was all you."

Ferd flailed for a moment, his paper fluttering in his hand. "I've never got a D for anything in my life. My father would…" And he paused there, not finishing the sentence. Holly and I did him the courtesy of pretending the first half of the sentence had never happened.

His father, one of the mighty Basilisks who represented all that was wealth and power at Belladonna U (not to mention the city as a whole) would not approve of the poetry course in the first place, but his father had little interest in anything Ferd did these days. Anything, that is, other than desperately seeking a cure for the laboratory accident that stripped a promising young Shadowmancy student of all magical powers one year ago.

Ferd claimed not to care about his father's opinions these days, but family programming was a hard thing to break.

"It's just one mark," I assured him. "There's another assignment before we get to the exam. You can make it up."

"If I miraculously grasp the point of villanelles during the week."

"Studying does not require miracles," I said, bringing out my inner starchy governess voice. "It requires elbow grease, endless cups of tea and an open mind."

"Oh," said Holly, smirking. "I wish you were my study partner."

I ignored her, which is the best way to deal with the confusing flirtatious note she has added to our banter in recent months. Holly has no romantic interest in me; that she has added me to the 75% of the population she is willing to flirt with has next to no meaning.

"You said you want to move outside your comfort zone this semester," I reminded Ferd. "You want to try new things, explore new fields that the old Ferdinand Chauvelin would never have considered. *Teach me your ways, Juniper*, you said. *You're my only hope, Juniper*, you said."

"I miss Shadowmancy," he said heavily. "Words have purpose in spell construction. Multiple purposes. Layers and function. They're not just… lying around in pretty patterns waiting for passers-by to admire them."

My voice rose beyond the socially appropriate levels for a library. "I'm sorry, you think poetry consists of *words lying around*? No wonder you got a D."

"Well, it's not *for* anything, is it?" Ferd glared at me. "It doesn't do anything useful."

Holly cackled at us both. I'd almost forgotten she was there.

(That's a lie. My awareness of Holly is constant and never-changing, like oxygen and the colour spectrum and the perfection that is Anne Brontë.)

"Why are you here?" I huffed, changing the subject.

Holly gave me an odd look, like she wasn't used to being questioned by me. That's… fair. The old me wouldn't say boo to a goose, and I used to hold back from sending anything like criticism in her direction.

I have more confidence these days. And I can't help but notice that the more I stand up to Holly, the more flirtation she adds to our banter.

It's not messing with my head at *all*.

"So," she said, clearing her throat. "Delightful poetry shenanigans aside, I wanted to ask you both to come home with me and Hebes for Halloween." And then with a complete disregard for proper grammar: "We're Halloweening. The full bit. Pumpkins and broomsticks. Didn't Hebe tell you?" she threw at Ferd, who looked confused, like this was the first he had heard of it.

"This is the first I've heard of it," said Ferd, clearly suspecting a trap. He might be lost around poetry, but he had the measure of Holly Hallow by now.

Holly smiled a delicious, sparkling smile. It did nothing for me.

(Obviously that was also a lie, see my previous statement about oxygen and Anne Brontë.)

"I'm sure she meant to," Holly assured him. It was a very trustworthy voice. She was good at those. "The Mums are excited. They can't wait to meet you."

She meant Ferd, not me. He was Hebe's boyfriend, after all, the one overdue to charm his way through the whole 'meet the family' gauntlet.

I knew that she didn't mean me.

But.

Holly being Holly, it completely sounded like she did.

CHAPTER FOUR
SAGE SETTLES FOR SECOND-RATE

THE MUDPIE WAS NOT my favourite chocolate joint. It wasn't even in the top three. But it was the nearest to uni that wasn't Cirque De Cacao, and I couldn't go there because, yet again, I'd made a dumb decision involving my dick.

I was drinking something called a cacao slammer, which had no caffeine in it, but not a whole lot of taste either. It was mostly grit with pretensions of grandeur in a too-small cup.

"What on earth are you doing here?"

I knew that affected posh-boy drawl so well by now, my skin prickled in response.

"What are *you* doing here?" I retorted as Jules Nightshade's shadow fell over mine. "I thought you were a five star only bloke. Coffee served with silk napkins and designer spoons."

"Not always," said Jules with a smirk that made my magic wake up and salute, damn it. I hated that my magic liked him so much. "Five stars are for hotels, not chocolate shops," he added. "And I'm pretty sure… this place does not have any stars." He sat opposite me, his stupidly expensive sunglasses resting on top of his stupid blond hair.

Okay, it was October, the weather was warming up. But still. Was that an excuse for Dolce and Gabbana sunnies?

I bit off the insult I was going to chuck his way because we were friends now, sort of. I was trying to be his mate, anyway, since being hatefuck hookups had gone badly for us, and the bloke needed more friends in his life who weren't straight.

We'd bitten off more than we could chew, signing up for the same class this semester. It brought out all our old rivalry. Fighting with him over method and theory and mythological magic was way more fun than it should be, and we were driving the rest of the class — and Vale in particular — out of their minds.

Still, I wasn't gonna be the first to admit it was a terrible idea.

Jules looked expectant.

"What?" I demanded.

"I was waiting for some kind of explanation as to why you're slumming it here when there's a perfectly good chocolate shop a block away." Jules took the cup off me, sniffed at it, and set it down with distaste. "I wouldn't feed that to a truffle hog."

"I don't have to explain myself to someone who knows what a truffle hog is," I muttered.

He raised his eyebrows. "Isn't that the sort of thing a friend would do?"

Well played. Jules was still poking and prodding at this new friendship of ours, trying to prove I wasn't for real.

I'd show him.

"Fine. I can't go back to Cirque De Cacao right now because I've done something really, really stupid."

Jules' eyes gleamed. "Tell me more."

"Nope nope nope."

"Ugh, well if you're not going to share gossip I suppose we can go straight to business."

Other parts of me woke up at that little invitation. Earlier in the year, back when we were hooking up all the time, phrases like 'straight to business' almost always meant 'where's the nearest bed and/or wall?' I had no idea what it meant now. "We have business?"

"Vale's class," said Jules. "We're being dicks."

"Yeah," I said slowly. "I know that. I didn't know *you* knew that."

Jules gave me a frosty look. "I happen to be an expert on me being a dick, and you've provided enough material over the last year that I can spot it in you from a distance."

"Fair enough. So, what's the plan?" Would the plan involve us getting naked to deal with the tension? I should not support that plan.

Parts of me were very enthusiastic about that plan.

Damn it. I was gonna need some caffeine if this conversation went on much longer. I could feel Jules' magic unfurling along his skin. I wanted to lick his neck.

Students get away with a lot around here but you gotta have some boundaries, and licking other people's necks was pretty high on my list of shit not to do in public when sober.

Jules gave me a weary 'so much more mature than you' expression that was uncalled for unless he was a fucken mindreader. "I didn't say we should hook up again."

"I didn't say you said that. Or that you think it. I have *no opinion* on this one."

Jules sighed. "I think we need to work together properly. The mid-semester project, the one due after Halloween? If we partner up and show her we can actually get something out of this course. It'd be, you know. Good."

His neck, which I was in no way paying attention to, went kind of pink. Aww. Was Nightshade embarrassed? Better him than me.

"You're a total teddy bear for that girl," I said with fierce glee. "You want to make her happy."

"Shut up, she's my friend." He stuttered a little over that last word because he was raised by expensive nannies or possibly frost giants.

"Okay," I conceded. "Teamwork. We can put a project together and make Viola proud and not have sex with each other. That sounds doable."

"That's what I thought," said Jules, awfully smug for someone who had just put way too much effort into scoring a good project partner for a mythology class. He smiled wide, like a Disney villain. "Now tell me about how stupid you have to be to get yourself banned from the best cafe in the area. Be my cautionary tale."

I let my head fall to the table. "Baristas, man. Don't date baristas. Especially when said baristas have equally hot, sarcastic twin brothers who dress in CONFUSINGLY SIMILAR STYLES."

"Sage," said Jules in a strangled voice. "Have you been dating twins? Again?"

So yeah. The amount of shit he heaped on me for that. I reckon we really are friends now. Go figure.

CHAPTER FIVE
HEBE IS BRAVE FOR ART

Dodecahedron has created this mirrorchat

Dodecahedron: Yo

The Nice Twin: you can't bring yo back, Dec. It's dead.

The Nice Twin: hang on

Dodecahedron: *[smirky goblin dance]*

The Nice Twin: Dec you have no magic how are you even on mirrorchat?

Meicakes: yooooo I regret nothing

The Nice Twin: you could have texted me like a normal person. Or called down the stairs since we live in the same house. Hang on, are you in Mei's room? You're like. Three feet away from me.

The Nice Twin: I CAN HEAR YOU TYPING

Dodecahedron: mirrorchat is wild, how do you even see the internet in this many dimensions?

Dodecahedron: the talking cats are kind of a pain though

The Nice Twin: oh Mei put you on the kindergarten setting. Nice.

Dodecahedron: I'd feel insulted if the talking cats hadn't just taught me to do this *[cauldron dance] [pumpkin dance] [disco frogs]*

The Nice Twin: whyyyy

Dodecahedron: *[newt] [newt] [newt metamorphoses into a unicorn]*

Dodecahedron: so Hebe I need a siren

The Nice Twin: the fire alarm is dodgy enough we don't need to add anything to it

Dodecahedron: for my art, duh. Can I draw you?

Meicakes: chiming in here to remind Hebe of the 'bucket list of brave' she planned to complete this FINAL semester of being a uni student

The Nice Twin: would I have to be, you know?

Dodecahedron: skyclad?

The Nice Twin: no witch says skyclad, ever. Except some of my great-aunts we don't talk to.

Dodecahedron: anyhoo only a little bit skyclad. I need back

muscles, shoulder, lots of hair. No boobs. V. Tasteful. No worries if you're not up for it…

The Nice Twin: I'll do it. For the Bucket List of Brave.

Meicakes: *[centaur dance] [amazon dance] [valkyries dancing with centaurs and amazons]*

Dodecahedron: that is some hardcore dancemoji action. Respect. But can you turn them off now? One of them just danced out of the mirror and up my nose…

THE POSE WAS NOT uncomfortable as such. Hebe sprawled on her front, over a heap of couch cushions, one arm outstretched.

It was being observed that did not feel comfortable or familiar. She knew Dec, and she trusted him, but she didn't think she'd be any less weirded out if she was wearing several jumpers instead of being bare from the waist up.

He had offered to take his shirt off too, if it made her feel better. She appreciated the thought but told him it might make things weird.

"You must be nearly done," she said aloud. He didn't need to sketch her face, at least; she didn't think she could have coped with that at all. "I mean, with your project."

Dec had spent his entire third year sculpting women as mythical monsters.

"Yep, this is the last piece," he said. "Still got to do a bunch of construction on my maenad installation — Mei's LGBTQ D&D group sat for it, and they were wild. I barely escaped alive."

"How thematically appropriate."

"I know, right?" He sounded pleased with himself. "They got so into it. Pretty sure they're gonna team up and do crimes now."

"So what happens next? I mean, with your project."

"It's all about the final end of year show. Gotta be as impressive as possible. They do the full bit — art critics and local patrons and all that. Fancy art shit. Then a very lucky handful get invited to do it again after graduation, only in the real world, with real money on the table."

"Sounds terrifying," Hebe said without thinking, but Dec laughed in his usual easy-going way.

"Sure. Still gotta be in it to win it."

"Why aren't you freaking out?" she asked. Somehow it was easier to ask questions like that when you weren't looking at a person, even if she knew he and his scritching pencil were scrutinising her, capturing every detail of her bare spine and shoulders. "It's our last semester, it's… I mean, it's almost over."

There was a rustling sound as Dec moved to another page. "I know I want to make art," he said. "I've learned a lot from the professors who aren't arseholes. I reckon that being an artist, really making a go of it — well, it's not gonna be that different to being a student. I'll still be living on instant noodles, still living here for as long as I can swing the cheap rent, still dating Viola if I'm lucky. I know how to do those things. Can you shift slightly on to your right hip?"

Hebe complied. "I feel stuck," she confessed. "Like I can't make decisions. At all. Ferd asked me what kind of muffin I wanted for breakfast the other day and I forgot all the options. I asked for cookies and cream!"

"First of all, shut up, cookies and cream muffins sound amazing, we should trademark the recipe right now."

"True enough."

"Also, I'm pretty sure you just have one decision to make right now, mate. Deadline to apply for Honours is what, two weeks away?"

"The Monday after Halloween," Hebe said dismally.

"Don't do this to yourself, Hebes. Fill in the form. You love being a uni student. You can take one more year, which opens up all those postgrad opportunities. Teaching, if you want to. That librarianship Masters, if you want to. A Doctorate, if you're not fussy about getting employed later on. And if you change your mind you can withdraw your app, or say no when they accept you."

Hebe's whole body tensed up. The idea of saying no if she was offered an Honours place was… impossible. How could she justify that? "I still have some thinking to do. Anyway, wouldn't doing Honours be a choice to put off other decisions about my future?"

"Ha," said Dec unsympathetically. "Throwing shade on every Hons student in the country, nice one. Except those who already know they want academia to swallow them whole forever like my brilliant girlfriend," he added hastily.

"Nice save."

"Yo, Dec," said a familiar voice from the kitchen. "You got a — holy fuck."

Hebe froze, remembering all of a sudden that she was topless. Damn it. Holly wouldn't care. Holly would be all 'excuse you, I happen to be naked here.' Hebe had no idea how to not worry what people thought of her. "Sage, don't you knock?" she wailed.

"This is literally my living room," said her best friend and ex-boyfriend, who hovering in the doorway, both hands slapped over his eyes. "Are you being art right now?"

"Well, I was. Now I'm being *really embarrassed*."

"Coffee break," sighed Dec. We can finish this later."

Hebe had always been faintly embarrassed that her domestic magic had a tendency to construct throw cushions and cups of tea in a crisis, but right now she appreciated it. When she sat up from her siren pose, it was with several throw cushions casually gathered in front of her like a bouquet.

"So uh," said Sage, hands still covering his eyes. "Halloweening. Just wanted to — yeah, I'm gonna wait in the kitchen until everyone's wearing clothes. Not that it's weird," he added quickly.

There was something about his discomfort that made Hebe feel a lot less awkward. She met Dec's eyes and he laughed, pulling off his Witches Roll Dice, Bitches t-shirt and chucking it to her.

She pulled it on — it was roomy and comfortable — and headed to the kitchen while a shirtless Dec followed her in.

"I feel so attacked right now," said Sage, at the coffee pot. "So uh, not to make it weird or anything, but do Vale and Ferd know you two are doing this?"

Hebe glared at him. "Sage, remember you asked me to tell you when you were accidentally being sexist and offensive?"

"It's not like it's even the first time me and Hebe have seen each other naked," Dec shrugged.

Hebe threw her hands up in despair.

Sage's mouth fell open.

"Okay," Dec admitted in the suddenly silent kitchen. "*Now* it's weird."

CHAPTER SIX
HEBE BLOWS HOLLY'S MIND

R0ckg0dde$$ has created this mirrorchat

R0ckg0dde$$: we're all going onna halloweeny holiday no more troubles for a day or three BUTTERNUT PUMPKIN FOR EVERYONE it is decided

Hebe So Boring: so um how many of our friends did you invite to the Mums for Halloween this year?

R0ckg0dde$$: ALLADEM!

R0ckg0dde$$: But Nora can't because bah family responsibilities whatevs

Hebe So Boring: I've made a list of those who have mentioned it to me, so far we're talking Sage, Dec, Ferd (my actual boyfriend thank you for deciding it was time he met my parents), Viola Vale, Jules Nightshade — are we friends with him now, when was that vote?, Mei, Juniper.

R0ckg0dde$$: yeeeeees sounds about right

Hebe So Boring: we have too many friends

Hebe So Boring: counting us that's nine people did you even give the mums a head's up about this? Has anyone thought of travel logistics? Sleeping arrangements? Groceries?

R0ckg0dde$$: it's gonna be so grayyyyyte

Hebe So Boring: *adds organising trip to to-do list, hates sister forever*

R0ckg0dde$$: so business as uush

Hebe So Boring: in other news, apparently Sage had no idea that Dec and I were hooking up last year. Did he miss the memo?

R0ckg0dde$$: wait what now

R0ckg0dde$$: *[mind blown dancemoji]*

R0ckg0dde$$: *[exploding earth dancemoji]*

R0ckg0dde$$: *[heat death of the universe dancemoji]*

R0ckg0dde$$: is slain from shock

Hebe So Boring: so in other news apparently NO ONE knew that Dec and I were hooking up last year. Do you think if I did crimes people would also not notice?

Hebe So Boring: seriously

Hebe So Boring: I mean, it was for like three months how did no one notice? It wasn't a secret.

Hebe So Boring: you knew though, right? Holly? You know everything

R0ckg0dde$$: ...

R0ckg0dde$$: everything I THOUGHT I knew is upside down, what was I even doing last year that I missed this?

Hebe So Boring: you weren't going to classes so *[minotaur shrugging dancemoji]*

R0ckg0dde$$: I didn't evnen know you knew what hookup meant arne't you basically a nun in a witch's hat?

Hebe So Boring: *[setting fire to witch's hat dancemoji]*

R0ckg0dde$$: huh this does explain how the rumour that I date nerds got started thanks for that

Hebe So Boring: your entire musical career is based on the implicit promise that you might date nerds

Hebe So Boring: nerds would be a step up from your last 3 boyfriends, by the way. Good nerds like Dec, not scary troll nerds who have opinions about whether The Bromancers is too gay now boys kiss in the show instead of staring longingly at each other in cars.

R0ckg0dde$$: hmm so would you provide him with a reference? Dec that is not the Bromancers boyzz I assume you have not been making out with them also

Hebe So Boring: my reference is one page typed neatly telling you that Dec is monogamously attached to Viola.

R0ckg0dde$$: is that still happening? Huh she seems the sort to set fire to his stuff and storm out at the eight week anniversary

R0ckg0dde$$: ok if they break up I totally want to make out with Viola, put that on my to do list, you keep that updated for me, right?

Hebe So Boring: *[repeated dancemoji of a witch swaying on the spot while hitting herself in the head with a pumpkin]*

PART TWO

HALLOWEENING

CHAPTER SEVEN
VIOLA AND HER BOYS GO A LITTLE BIT COUNTRY

"So," said Viola Vale, looking over her sunglasses at her two best friends. "Meet the parents."

"*I'm* not meeting anyone's parents," said Jules Nightshade over a steaming decaf cinnamon latte.

Viola coughed her amusement into a napkin. "Keep telling yourself that, babe."

Ferdinand Chauvelin rolled his eyes at them both, bit into his almond biscotti, and said nothing.

The three of them had opted to fly together to the touristy mountain town where Hebe and Holly's mothers apparently ran a successful homemade candle business, surrounded by extended family, witchy traditions going back hundreds of years, and... well, a lot of bees and sheep, probably.

Viola had been a city girl her whole life; she had no idea how the country worked.

Travelling by broomstick meant at least that all three took themselves out of the 'how many people can we fit in the band van' challenge that their friends and significant others were still arguing about when they left.

It also gave Viola some breathing space to face the upcoming holiday. Halloween for her meant fancy black tie events hosted by her father, or Nightshade's parents, or Chauv's. Halloween meant the three of them sneaking away to drink stolen vodka, setting jinxes to prank their least favourite guests.

This year, Victor Vale made no mention of any Halloween social commitments, and he barely reacted when Viola mentioned going out of town with her friends.

Was she officially uninvited from the fancy side of town now that Chauv was on the outs with his family? Or was there something else going on she had no idea about?

"Do you know what your mother is doing this year?" she asked Nightshade, lightly enough that he wouldn't think the answer mattered.

She clearly hadn't been subtle enough; Chauv sent her a glower from behind his cup.

"Some kind of retreat," Jules shrugged. "Cucumber baths and rose petal charms as part of her overall campaign to pretend she's not turning fifty."

Viola blinked. "She doesn't turn fifty for another three years."

"She's taking a run up at pretending it's not happening."

A flock of children ran past the cafe in costumes: super-heroes and monsters and a few cartoony witches from favourite TV shows, the kind with fake warts and striped green stockings.

Viola winced. "School's out, then. We should get going. We said we'd be there by four."

"I don't know about you," said Jules, "but I don't want to risk turning up before the others, do you?" He eyed the menu.

"One more drink," Viola conceded. "But don't you dare sneak in any actual coffee. I'm not hauling you along on the back of my broomstick. If you dampen your magic, you can walk the rest of the way."

She winced and looked at Chauv.

The downside of travelling by broomstick was that it brought his lack of magic into the foreground, instead of stuffed into the back of the closet of topics they never talked about. Viola was steering his broomstick remotely, using a charm usually reserved for children and unlicensed flyers. It was, he had decided, slightly less mortifying for him than having to ride along behind one of his friends on the same broom.

Viola needn't have worried about her clanger. Chauv wasn't listening to her at all, staring into the distance.

"Hey," she said to get his attention. "Lover boy. Not freaking out about this, are you?"

Chauv gave her a weak smile. "Well it's not like Hebe's parents can hate me more than mine do right now…"

"Self pity fine," said Jules, stealing the rest of the biscotti. "You know what you did," he added sternly, and crammed them all into his mouth.

Chauv laughed at that. "You know," he teased. "Speaking of meeting the parents, I'm pretty sure Hebe's mums are the closest thing that Sage McClaren has to family…"

Jules rolled his eyes while crunching his mouthful of biscotti. "Imagine how much I don't care."

IT WAS A FARM. An actual farm. Viola was glad she had thought to wear boots instead of heels, but regretted the fact that she hadn't had the foresight to wear less awesome boots. Hers were going to get wrecked.

"This is like something out of a book," said Jules, as their broomsticks all hovered near the bright red letterbox with HALLOW scrawled on the side. "A disaster novel," he added, in case any of them forgot for ten seconds that he was a dedicated snob.

"The van's here, at least," said Chauv, pointing up the meandering driveway to the Fake Geek Girl band van parked in front of an enormous barn, which did indeed look like something out of a book — a children's picture book about chickens, possibly.

"Splendid," said Viola. "That's sure to make things less awkward." She hesitated for a moment because why were they even here again?

Chauv bounced anxiously on his broomstick, tugging at Viola's steering charm — oh that's right, meet the parents, this was rather more of an investment for him than it was for Viola and Jules. Taking pity on him, she sent him careening up ahead of them, following close behind. Jules followed sullenly. Where else was he going to go?

There were Halloween garlands up and down the driveway, culminating in a full explosion of black cats, pumpkins and witch hats draped over the outside of the charming weatherboard farmhouse.

Jules stared at it all in fascination, as if he had never seen anything tacky before in his life — a bluff, because the student bar had been dripping in cheap Halloween tat for weeks already.

Chauv hesitated at the doorway. Viola took over, pushing him all the way forward to knock and, at the cheerful call from inside, to enter.

If Halloween had exploded outside, it then proceeded to sneeze all over the inside of the house. They found themselves in an enormous, sunny kitchen full of beeswax tallow, butternut pumpkins, and hanging lanterns reflecting every Halloween cliche in bouncing patterns of paper.

Familiar faces and complete strangers were all jammed into the kitchen together, many of them sorting bowls full of lollies or performing strange cooking rituals, and others drinking cups of tea, laughing, chatting.

It was Viola's idea of hell; like one of her father's awful parties except where everyone involved actually liked each other, and had no concept of personal space.

Dec swooped at them moments before Holly, which was something of a relief. Viola found herself steered widdershins around the kitchen by her boyfriend, while Chauv and Jules were dragged off clockwise. She was introduced to several people who hugged her, bowed politely in formal witch-style, or in the case of those who already knew her, offered ironic high-fives and/or pretended to be people with different names who did indeed need to be introduced.

Finally she spotted Jules and Chauv again. They looked as shell-shocked as she felt. They were wedged in a corner together, on the far side of the kitchen. Chauv was holding a plate of gingerbread broomsticks, and Jules was holding a cup of mint tea like he wanted to stab someone with it.

"Back in a sec, V," Dec said in Viola's ear. He kissed her on the cheek and then hurried off to help Sage turn a large table into, apparently, an even larger table, without the use of magic. They were just… folding wood. Viola stared in amazement.

"Get me out of here," Jules whispered with a frantic, terrified smile. "They're all so *nice*."

Chauv had wiped all expression from his face, which made him look faintly bored if you didn't know him at all. "Either I miscounted," he murmured to Viola. "Or Hebe has three mothers. *Three*. How did I not know that? You'd think that's the sort of thing that comes up in conversation!"

Viola decided then and there that she was going to enjoy herself this weekend. She leaned in, and took a gingerbread broomstick off the plate. "Happy Halloween, darlings."

CHAPTER EIGHT
MISS JUNIPER'S RECIPE FOR DISASTER (EVERYTHING TASTES BETTER WITH PUMPKIN)

THERE IS an odd discomfort in being a witch in the Southern Hemisphere. Despite the best efforts of grass roots campaigns, there is little mainstream acceptance of the idea that rotating our traditional holidays would make oh, so much sense.

So we live our lives upside down, constantly reminded that we are Other. We leap the Beltane fires as autumn gets dark, and we attend Yule Balls at the height of summer.

Halloween in Australia is a Spring festival, believe it or not, because that's what October looks like. It's bright, sunny and warm. Trick or Treating children race around screaming with their sugar high well past 8pm, when the sun is only just beginning to dim thanks to daylight savings.

Pumpkins are not in season.

Oh, you wouldn't know it to look at our supermarkets and grocery stores. October is a month of pumpkins for sale. They spill up over display racks and end up in shopping carts for no good reason. There's an entire farming industry dedicated to providing pumpkins out of season, when they taste especially watery and bland, because October is when witches want to carve pumpkins, and display them on their porches.

Butternut pumpkins, though. That's another matter. Not even the most magical and committed Australian farmer can make a carving pumpkin taste good at the wrong end of the year. But since the 90's, there has been a great deal of success with butternut pumpkins in spring.

The witching community is divided every year between those witches who cook dozens of holiday recipes featuring actually-delicious-at-this-time-of-year butternut pumpkins, those witches who declare that butternut is cheating and only the bleh out-of-season pumpkins are worth cooking because TRADI-TION OVER TASTE... not to mention that third faction of charming denialists who want to inform us every year that no matter how many witches there are practicing in this country, Halloween isn't something Australians should celebrate, because American culture is ruining everything, and in their day you celebrated All Hallows with two candles and a boiled egg.

Ahem.

The Hallows, it turned out, were sensible butternut witches. Their kitchen smelled delicious, of roast vegies and cinnamon. Agatha Hallow, one of Hebe and Holly's mothers, presided over the holiday cooking like the goddess of the hearth posing on the front cover of the Australian Women's Weekly Seasonal Desserts Special Issue. Agatha's wild grey-brown hair was tangled up into a festive arrangement of silk leaves and fresh wattle flower. She also had half of a gingerbread broomstick tucked into her snood; I wasn't sure if this was deliberate and so chose not to mention it to anyone.

Desiree Hallow, whom I was pretty sure was the mother actually descended from the famous Hallow line by birth, was a tall and stately witch with raven black hair and a grim expression. She was the task mistress who kept everything spinning along despite there being so many different recipes, jobs and projects to manage, and so many people in the house that it made my head hurt.

Despite her lack of smiles and welcoming warmth, I could see something of Hebe in Desiree — she had a knack for sensing when one of her guests (me, more than once) was getting over-whelmed, and she would come up with some sort of simple, doable task to get us (me, mostly) out of the kitchen and away from the crowd, for a few moments at least.

Then there was Sophonisba. A redhead with a sturdy figure and eye-watering dress sense (so many baubles and clashing tie-dyed colours), Sophonisba Hallow was a whirlwind of chaos and creativity.

Sage was her favourite. Sage, when I came to pay attention, was clearly doted upon by all three of the Hallow mums, which made sense. I got the impression he had spent his younger teen years starving for a family, and the Hallows provided in cauldrons.

No one was paying a great deal of attention to me now, while I performed my current 'make yourself useful' task of chopping pumpkins which were to be roasted and souped, skin and all. That's how I liked it. You learn a lot from being quietly unobserved.

The Hallow mums were doing their due and solemn diligence when it came to meet-the-parents duty, which meant finding space in the chaos to thrust childhood photo albums at Ferd, and ask him pointed questions he never quite managed to answer (they had been worded up, clearly, not to ask about his parents, but they did not hold back when it came to his university options, his future plans, and his opinion on every butternut pumpkin recipe they put in front of him). When Sage wasn't looking, Agatha pushed at least one 'awkward teen years' album at Jules, who looked startled and embarrassed but accepted the gesture as the fuel for mockery that it was.

Sage didn't seem to notice the teasing, though it was sure to pay off later as Viola observed the whole scene and was snickering in the corner, making Jules' ears go red. Sage followed Sophonisba around, hanging decorations at her command, and chatting cheerfully about some project or other. It took me a while to notice that he wasn't just hanging off this particular Hallow mum because they were especially fond of each other, but because he was avoiding Hebe.

Hebe was pissed off at Sage. She rolled her eyes at him whenever he accidentally made eye contact with her, which was out of character for her. Dec was avoiding both of them, even more out of character. Holly was impatient with all three of them, and when Holly thinks you're being immature, it should sound all kinds of warning sirens.

Once you see a fracture in the social group that, for reasons of music and friendship, you are bonded to for life, it's hard to unsee it. It unsettled me. I came from a family that never fought fair, and put in very little effort to hang on to me after I left home. That's why I hate fighting so much.

Whenever Holly and Sage blow up at each other, part of me always frets that this is the fight that will ruin things forever. Break up the band. End the friendships. Burn the found family to the ground. I never feel safe, even though they forgive each other so thoroughly and sincerely every single time. (How do they do that?)

This afternoon, when my chopped pumpkins were whisked away for the next stage of their Halloween journey, I waited in hope to be given another of those 'pop outside for a minute, love' tasks from Desiree, but one didn't come fast enough.

Some local kids in festive zombie outfits arrived at the kitchen door just in time. Holly and Sage bickered over which of them got to hand out over-generous handfuls of lollies to the trick or treaters, and Viola got into an argument with Dec about whether Trick or Treating was an American tradition or not, and what place it should hold in the Australian Halloween.

It turned out that their argument was actually the two of them agreeing with each other very loudly. Finally they both said in unison "as long as no one calls it candy" and then burst out laughing.

That was my moment. I backed into the main house, leaving nothing behind me but a handful of pumpkin seeds in a novelty tea towel.

The living room was quiet, despite the muffled noise from the kitchen. I made it through the long weatherboard house, past the staircase that was clearly a modern addition to the building, and all the way through the house to the candle workshop, rich with the scent of beeswax, tallow and air-drying herbs.

A door led out to the verandah. All-around verandahs are a great Australian tradition, providing all kinds of helpful nooks and impromptu seating for introverts who need five minutes to themselves.

"There you are!" a deep voice lurched at me from across the workshop.

I leapt in the air, almost braining myself on a giant pineapple-scented wheel of wax. "What the — aargh! Cello," I said, blurting out the excuse I had ready if anyone asked where I was going. "Need to — check, retune — Ferd, *what*?"

Yes, it was Ferd. He looked rough around the edges, far too stressed for someone who had been force fed cups of tea and family photo albums for the last couple of hours.

Or maybe, exactly that amount of stressed.

"Juniper," he said in a hoarse voice, grabbing hold of my arm. "I need to talk to you about poetry."

CHAPTER NINE
BONFIRE REAL TALKS

Hebe So Boring has created this mirrorchat

Hebe So Boring: you have to help me

R0ckg0dde$$: you actually identify as Hebe So Boring now? What have I done to you & how can I weaponise it against other people

R0ckg0dde$$: also using mirrorchat at a family gathering instead of being goody two shoes and 'yes I will admire this bonfire for 3 hours' I am so proud rite now

R0ckg0dde$$: is this about Sage going all big brother and weird on you about your sexual conquest revelations cos I will beat him with a butternut pumpkin if necess

Hebe So Boring: its about Ferd

Hebe So Boring: but if you want to hit Sage with a butternut pumpkin I would not be averse

————

R0ckg0dde$$ has created this mirrorchat

R0ckg0dde$$: Sage, stop being a fuckwit

FuçxkW1tPrime: Holly???

R0ckg0dde$$: u don't get to be possessive about Hebe it's WEIRD DUDE don't do it

R0ckg0dde$$: your better than this

FuçxkW1tPrime: I'm not being weird and possessive

FuçxkW1tPrime: Hebe's the one being weird around me

R0ckg0dde$$: DO I HAVE TO PULL THIS BROOMSTICK OVER

R0ckg0dde$$: omg how drunk is my mum right now I think she's flirting with Jules look DON'T LOOK now look

FuçxkW1tPrime: she's squeezing his bicep omg SOphonisba no

R0ckg0dde$$: why is there no dancemoji for shame spiral

FuçxkW1tPrime: see Ferd rescued him problem solved

R0ckg0dde$$: now she is flirting with Ferd OMG this is everytihng/ is Hebe missing this? Best bonfire ever

R0ckg0dde$$: anyway back to th issh

FuçxkW1tPrime: I'm not talking to you about this

R0ckg0dde$$: whatever, but when it's ME shaming you for your behaviour? Gotta worry mate.

FuçxkW1tPrime: there was no behaviour! I barely reacted

R0ckg0dde$$: so why is Hebe upset?

FuçxkW1tPrime: because I'm the worst

R0ckg0dde$$: there you go

Dodecahedron has created this mirrorchat

Dodecahedron: maaate not cool

DrummersDoItLikeDikcheads: it's not weird I'm not being weird you're being weird

DrummersDoItLikeDikcheads: I think I preferred it when Holly set my Mirrorchat ID to FuçxkW1tPrime

Dodecahedron: your wish is my command

FuçxkW1tPrime: I DON'T CARE THAT YOU AND HEBE USED TO HOOK UP

Meicakes: whoa tone it down fam

FuçxkW1tPrime: Mei why are you here

Meicakes: it's my mirror

Dodecahedron: McClaren you two broke up like twelve years ago

FuçxkW1tPrime: nearly 3 years

Dodecahedron: reality check is not helping you here

FuçxkW1tPrime: this isn't an ex boyfriend thing. It's a friend thing AND ITS BARELY EVEN A THING

Meicakes: *[judgy eyebrows dancemoji]*

FuçxkW1tPrime: wtf did you custom make that one?

Meicakes: *[judgy eyebrows dancemoji with pride flag]*

———

Dodecahedron has created this mirrorchat

Dodecahedron: Hey V

V_is_for_vixen: I'm not having mirrorsex with you on Mei's mirror. Get your own.

Dodecahedron: wait that's a thing?

V_is_for_vixen: name one piece of human tech that can't be used for sex

Dodecahedron: we are so getting back to this later

Meicakes: I can sort you with the right gear

Dodecahedron: PRIVACY SETTINGS ALSO

Meicakes: well if you must

Dodecahedron: So, Viola you don't care that I used to sleep with Hebe like a year ago, do you? We never did the list of exes thing

V_is_for_vixen: which one is Hebe again?

Dodecahedron: that's what I thought

V_is_for_vixen: did you want to do the list of exes thing? I can but I have to check with my lawyer first because of non-disclosure agreements

Dodecahedron: wait what

V_is_for_vixen: some of them are celebrities

Dodecahedron: I regret everything about this conversation

Meicakes: OK he's gone Vi tell me everything

———

R0ckg0dde$$ has created this mirrorchat

R0ckg0dde$$: wait we forgot to talk about the Ferd thing

Hebe So Boring: that was four drinks and three hours and like, half a bonfire ago. I am not listening to your relationship advice right now

R0ckg0dde$$: Im practically sober

Hebe So Boring: I just saw you drink vodka out of a hollowed-out butternut pumpkin

R0ckg0dde$$: to be fair half of that was marshmallows

R0ckg0dde$$: I can't talk to you about relationship stuff when you're sober you get all uptight and closed off

Hebe So Boring: I've had two ciders, I am not the drunk one here.

Hebe So Boring: I think Ferd is going to break up with me

Hebe So Boring: Holly?

Hebe So Boring: where did you go?

———

SageMcClaren has created this mirrorchat

SageMcClaren: wanna get out of here and blow off some steam?

JulesNightshade: I'm not blowing anything in a house with this many nosy mothers in it

SageMcClaren: Ha, I didn't mean that. *[Cool sunglasses dance-moji]* There's no coffee at the Hallow house and if I don't siphon off some magic soon things are gonna get explosive.

JulesNightshade: so?

SageMcClaren: so I had an idea for our project

JulesNightshade: did you invite me to this party to do homework with you?

SageMcClaren: no you wanker my friends invited you to this party because they're weirdly attached to you and they think I like you like this is a high school dance party and you want to hold my hand

JulesNightshade: spellcasting drunk is a terrible idea

SageMcClaren: I'm not drunk you're drukn

JulesNightshade: of course I'm drunk. I'm in the middle of Nowheretown Hicksville and the glasses keep filling up with cider

SageMcClaren: yeah they do that

JulesNightshade: I ate a cookie with I think more booze in it than my mother's festive punch bowl

JulesNightshade: and then I ate more cookies

SageMcClaren: bro

SageMcClaren: mate

SageMcClaren: dude

SageMcClaren: lets do magic

JulesNightshade: fine but I'm keeping my pants on

SageMcClaren: *[pants dancemoji]*

CHAPTER TEN

HEBE AND VIOLA RECOMMEND YOU NOMINATE A DESIGNATED SPELLCASTER BEFORE EVERYONE STARTS DRINKING

HEBE SHOULD HAVE KNOWN BETTER than to admit anything to Holly, especially right now at the height of the booze-and-bonfire portion of Halloween, surrounded by friends and family.

Her sister grabbed her by the sleeve and yoinked her away from the crowd, towards the barn where they and their friends were supposed to be sleeping tonight.

(Hebe was certain that they were all relying on her annoyingly domestic magic to make things comfortable, but no one had actually asked her to provide beds, blankets and copious amounts of throw pillows — and she wasn't going to lift a finger until they did)

(Who was she kidding, she could practically hear the farm tools transforming into luxury sleeping bags thanks to her mere presence)

"Tell me everything," said Holly, pinning Hebe to the barn wall underneath a chain of glittery paper lanterns shaped like bats and owls. The Hallow family had gone all out with the crafting portion of Halloween this year. "Why do you think Ferd is breaking up with you, and when can I murder him?"

"Holly, we've been through this, you're not allowed to murder people for breaking up with me," said Hebe. She attempted a joke: "Hey, some of our best friends have broken up with me."

"I will kill everyone at this party if I have to," her sister promised with a disturbing intensity.

Hebe closed her eyes, letting herself not be cheerful for a brief moment. It felt liberating. "Ferd has been avoiding me, he shuts down any conversations about the future, and those are the only conversations I want to have with anyone right now because hello, I'm running out of time to make all these huge decisions and…" She stopped and took a few deep breaths because the alternative was going looking for a paper bag to blow into.

Holly made eye contact with her sister. "Does he think you're sleeping with Sage and/or Dec?"

"No!" Hebe couldn't believe Holly would even say that. "Why would he think that? Why would anyone think that?"

"That's the sort of thing people accuse *me* of before they break up with me."

"Holly," Hebe sighed. "Usually you *are* sleeping with other people."

"That's not the point! The point is…" Holly's voice trailed off. "I'm so thirsty."

"Maybe we can talk about this more when you're sober? Or not ever again?"

"Can you smell..?" Holly tipped her head to one side. "What is that *smell*?"

Hebe might have known her sister's attention span would be at its worst right now. Some help she turned out to be. "All I smell is candles and bonfire. And cider. Your breath is rank right now."

The air rippled around them.

"Someone's doing some kind of —" the word was *spell*, Hebe could hear it forming in the air as she lost all sound. Her ears popped with the pressure of… not just magic.

Big magic. Familiar magic. Magic that tasted like nostalgia and warm hugs and Sage making bad decisions.

She pushed Holly, screaming for her to get out of the way, but there was no sound, there was no…

There was no Holly.

Hebe lurched forward and hit a wall of hay. Spun around and… more hay. She was blocked in by walls of haybales, higher than her head, and only one way out.

There wasn't *any* hay harvested at this time of year. It was spring. This smelled like freshly dried pea straw, the good stuff that the Mums bought in for mulching, and there was never more than a few bales of it around the property at a time.

Hebe hurried on, twisting and turning. She went down three dead ends before she realised what was going on here.

She was trapped in a hay maze.

———

VIOLA HAD ALMOST MANAGED to relax. She lay with her head on Dec's shoulder, watching the casual family chaos around her — why did the Hallows have so many cousins — with the warm burn of home-brew cider in her stomach, and a sticky bowl of dried apple chips at her elbow.

For a few seconds she stopped thinking about curriculum and footnotes and her dread thesis. For a few seconds, she stopped worrying about what her friends were up to.

That was clearly a mistake on her part.

There was a whooshing sound, and Viola's ears popped with the pressure of high intensity magic performed without proper safety procedures.

Viola blinked. The bonfire was cold. Dec sprawled out on the dirt under her, flattened like a freshly-punched scarecrow.

"Dec!" He was out cold, and would not rouse.

There was a hubbub around the fire. Several of the guests had vanished. Others leaned over other unconscious friends and family members, just like Dec.

Viola caught the eye of one of the Hallow Mums, the tall one with black hair and an icy expression.

"Is it all the people with low magic levels?" Viola asked.

Desiree Hallow nodded, looking grimmer than ever. "Do you know what happened here?"

Viola looked over her shoulder. The barn and the house had

both disappeared behind high walls of what looked like ancient stone, and bales of hay. The new walls were painted brightly, with Minoan frescos and gleaming mosaic tiles. All very classical, down to the ancient graffiti.

"I have a horrible feeling," Viola said wearily. "That Sage and Jules decided *now* was a good time to get their homework done."

CHAPTER ELEVEN
DOS AND DON'TS IN THE WAKE OF DISASTER

SAGE

YEAH IT WAS a stupid thing to do but all the pieces came together so well, a tidy piece of magic. We work well together, me and Nightshade.

I might've underestimated how powerful we actually are when we combine my magic and his. I definitely underestimated how compatible his magic would be with mine — who saw that coming?

Viola's gonna kill us.

Hebe's gonna kill us.

The Mums are gonna…

Yeah, maybe I should just stay in this maze forever.

———

JULES

Everything is McClaren's fault. If I knew where he was I would punch him in his stupid kissable mouth.

Why is there so much hay?

I hate the country.

HOLLY & JUNIPER

"Why is it a maze and why can't I find my sister?"

"Holly, is that you? I can hear you through the wall."

"Yes! Junie, are you on the outside? Is everyone freaking out?"

"They totally are. Are you okay?"

"Listen, Juniper, this is serious. There are a lot of witches in my family and they always want to be the one who solves the problem. This thing is — it feels really unstable. I need you to keep everyone calm and stop them throwing any more magic at this whole disaster. "

"Why me? I can't — what makes you think I can do that?"

"Because you're the calm and sensible one."

"No I'm not, I'm just shy!"

"Well, you have a calming effect on me."

"I do?"

"You can do this. I believe in you."

———

MEI & VIOLA

"This is Meicakes Central, liveblogging from the site of a Halloween disaster. A giant temple thing has appeared, many of my friends are missing, and only the magical people are awake. This is bad news, because all the awake magical people are heading for the temple — wall — did someone say maze? ready to throw a bunch of spells at it."

"Mei, stop live-streaming and follow me right now! We're going in."

"Vi, that's cute, but I'm more of an observer not a doer."

"Bring your mirror, and leave your attitude in that bag of marshmallows."

"My attitude *is* a bag of marshmallows."

"If there was anyone else I could ask to help me save the day believe me, I would not pick you."

"Your *face* is a bag of marshmallows…"

CHAPTER TWELVE

HEBE THEORISES THAT
PRACTICAL MYTHOLOGY IS
MORE EFFECTIVE WHEN
YOU'VE DONE THE
READINGS

HEBE TRIED FLYING over the walls, but the maze hated magic, or her, or both.

So she ran, twisting and turning, until the hay walls turned into painted stone covered in ancient graffiti, then back to hay, sometimes packed into walls alongside butternut pumpkins.

She didn't find her boyfriend so much as she tripped over him, and landed hard on the ground with Ferd's unconscious body cushioning her fall. "Oof!"

Ferd didn't seem to have anything wrong with him, but he wouldn't wake up however much Hebe shook him, or yelled in his ear.

"What do I do now?" she asked him hopelessly.

"When in doubt, make out with the unconscious person," said a sarcastic voice behind her. "Magic laughs in the face of consent ethics."

Hebe whirled around and threw herself at the comforting presence of Sage, all huggable shoulders wrapped up in flannel. "I'm so glad you're here," she said, clutching at him. "Wait, this is all your fault."

"It's like, forty percent my fault," Sage admitted.

She shoved away from him. "You smell like a craft brewery."

"That's cos I'm craft wasted," he said, and laughed like he found himself hilarious.

Hebe didn't. "I can't believe you were spellcasting *drunk*."

"It shouldn't have been a problem," Sage protested. "I've done it before with no drama. But Jules —" He paused, and looked around. "Hey, whoa. Nightshade was here a minute ago. I guess he went left when I went right, or I went left and he went right…"

"If you say you spellcast better when you've been drinking, I'm going to hit you with my unconscious boyfriend," Hebe said icily. "What were you thinking?"

Sage sagged, and dropped to the ground beside Ferd. "Clearly I wasn't thinking. Sorry, Hebes."

"Ugh," she said to him. "Why are you the worst?"

He shrugged and looked pitiful.

They did not appear to be in any imminent danger of being attacked by anything except haybales and butternut pumpkins.

With a sigh, Hebe lowered herself to sit next to Sage. "Why were you so spun out about this Dec revelation? This extremely old news?"

"I wasn't —" he huffed and started again. "Look, apart from the thing where you two are apparently super comfortable with your shirts off —"

"It was for art!"

"— I wasn't spun out, and I definitely wasn't being a dick," he complained. "I was working really hard not to —"

"There we go," said Hebe.

"What?" He did look confused, bless him. Clearly the magic hadn't siphoned off all the honey mead or whatever else he'd been drinking.

"Why did you have to work so hard at not being spun out? You know I've dated since you. Is it because I had casual sex for once in my life, or because it was your roommate, or… wait, *are you in love with Dec?*" Stranger things had happened.

"No! None of those things are — oh fuck, Hebe." Sage was clearly not at the correct alcohol level to deal with any of these suggestions. His head fell forward into his large hands. "What the hell?" he muttered.

"This is why we have conversations about things, so I don't make up whole new problems," she said sweetly.

"It was because I didn't know about it," he muttered.

"Am I supposed to ask permission? Put a guestbook by my bed for you to sign off on every weekend…"

Sage made a strangled screaming sound into his hands.

Hebe patted him on the knee. "Sorry, but you knocked my boyfriend unconscious with a giant homework project, I have to punish you a little."

"Do you, though?"

"I think we both know the answer to that."

"You're my best friend," he blurted out. "Or you would be if we were in primary school…"

"Grown ups are allowed to have best friends, Sage, move on."

"We've been at uni nearly 3 years and you were so chill about the break up, about the band… you come to every gig, you know everything that's happened to me, every hook up, every boyfriend, every —" He stopped and waved a hand wildly at the maze around them.

"Every incident that belongs in the Jules Nightshade Memorial Dossier of Bad Choices?" said Hebe.

"That. And I'm starting to think I've been a really crappy friend to you because I don't know half the stuff you've been doing…"

Hebe let out her own strangled scream.

Sage looked at her in surprise. "What?"

"This isn't on you, Sage," she snapped. "You didn't know about Dec because *I didn't tell you.* I mean, yes, we both assumed you knew — but I still didn't make an effort to discuss it with you. There's a lot of things I don't tell you. I know everything about your life because you are literally incapable of keeping secrets. When you figured out you were gay you ran to my doorstep to let me know as soon as possible."

"Well, yeah…"

"I keep things from you. A lot of things. I keep things from everyone."

Sage was looking at her now, his eyes soft and warm. Not even a little bit hurt, which was something. "Things like what?"

"I wasn't actually chill about the break up," she blurted out. "It kind of wrecked me. It took a really long time to get over it, and I never wanted you to see how much work it took…"

Sage was still staring at her, but his gaze wasn't warm any more. "See, I knew that."

"Because Holly told you. I never actually, you know. Said the words. Even after we both knew that you knew."

His face softened. "Holly never used the word *wrecked*."

"I'm fine now," Hebe said quickly.

"I know you're fine. You're brilliant. You're the best person I know."

"There you are!" said a voice, breaking into the moment. "What the hell happened?"

Hebe and Sage jolted upwards, staring at the newcomers — Viola, in her elegant semi-formal witch robes, and Mei wearing a pair of glasses shaped like humorous ghosts. Viola was holding a ball of string which unwound behind them like… oh, like the story of the labyrinth. That made sense.

"Your mate Jules Nightshade happened," said Sage automatically, which earned him an appropriately scornful glare from Viola.

"Is there a minotaur in here?" Hebe blurted out as the thought occurred to her. "Is that a thing that's happening?" She paused. "Did a minotaur eat Jules?"

"I'm not ruling it out," said Sage.

Viola, nearly a head shorter than him, leaned in and flicked him hard in the middle of the forehead. "You are a waste of magic," she informed him.

The maze shuddered around them and the passage was suddenly a lot more intimate than it had been.

"Is this place shrinking?" Mei asked in alarm.

"Oh no," said Hebe. She could feel the magic around them, squeezing inwards. She knew the scent of it, like she could tell which of her mothers had made any given batch of pumpkin scones. The maze didn't just smell like the unsettlingly pleasant combo of Sage McClaren and Jules Nightshade's magic any more. "I think the Mums are trying to break the spell."

"Yeah no, that's not gonna fly," said Sage frantically. "I love the Mums, but we put some hardcore advanced charmwork into this installation, and adding more magic on top of it is going to..."

The maze rippled and a loud roaring sound came from somewhere.

Viola closed her eyes. "You set trap hexes," she moaned. "Of course you did."

"This was our assignment, we wanted to impress you," said Sage.

The wall behind them, mostly made of butternut pumpkins and straw, burst into flames. Viola jumped and extinguished the fire with a word, but then stared in dismay as the wall hissed angrily at her.

The air filled with the scent of scorched pumpkin.

"Now I'm hungry," said Mei.

Hebe shoved at Sage. "Run. Go. Follow that string out of the maze and shut the Mums down. We'll bring Jules out, find anyone else stuck in here, sober you two up and get you to dissolve the charmwork properly."

"This is why you're our manager," he said, and did finger guns at her.

"I'm not the band's manager," she insisted. If she said it enough, it might be true.

Sage grinned widely. "Who said anything about the band?"

As Sage ran off, Viola crouched down beside the unconscious Ferd. "Everyone without magic — or extremely low magic, like Dec — lost consciousness when the maze hit."

"Likely it drew energy from everyone," said Mei. "But they had less to give.".

Viola shook her head grimly. "Shit. How much magic did they *use* on this thing?"

"How much do they have?" Hebe asked rhetorically. It was

something she had lowkey been thinking about for a while now. Both boys had stupid amounts of juice.

"Bad news," said Sage, returning with a sick expression on his face. "The maze is sealed up. All dead ends that way."

Another wave of magic sparked overhead. The maze rippled precariously under their feet.

"You mean it's changing?" Viola stood up, furious. She waved a finger at Sage. "If you knew anything about mazes of actual Minoan history, you'd know they were a spiral. One path, easy to get in and out of. They were fucking symbolic. And here we are, in a nightmare of David Bowie in *Labyrinth* proportions. Without the adorable Muppet goblins. Where are my Muppet goblins, McClaren?"

"I love that movie," Mei sighed. "I could be at home right now watching that movie if you all didn't make me commit to socialising in person."

There was a roar from somewhere within the maze.

"It's a bit worse than that," said Sage in a pained voice.

"You made a worse mess than even I think you made?" Viola demanded. "Not possible."

"Jules wasn't eaten by a minotaur," Sage confessed, all in a rush. Viola closed her eyes, like she knew what he was about to say. "The minotaur *is* Jules."

CHAPTER THIRTEEN
MINOTAURS HAVE TO LIVE SOMEWHERE

JULES NIGHTSHADE WAS PISSED off and cranky and sore and nothing really made sense right now. He had…

The magic had gone wrong, he knew that. The magic twisted him up in knots and turned him into this big, lumbering thing that couldn't walk in a straight line.

The booze was not helping.

His head was muzzy and thick, and there was only one thought clear in his entire head.

Kill Sage.

———

VIOLA WAS PANICKING.

She did not panic very often. She prided herself on being cool, calm, collected, impeccably dressed and ready for anything.

When it came to powerful magic…

Well.

A year or so ago, if something like this happened, she would have known exactly what to do. She would have punched Chauv on the arm and said, *fix this*, because she happened to be BFFS with one of the most talented young shadowmancers of his generation, and this shit? This had shadowmancy all over it.

"How can you have performed a magical act this big without knowing how to unravel it?" she demanded of Sage, who looked like he was sobering up very fast. "You always leave a thread to pull, that's basic charmcraft."

"Not when you're so powerful you don't bother to think about conserving energy or safety precautions because that's for mere mortals," said Hebe in an exhausted voice.

Sage shot her a wounded expression, but his friend merely raised an eyebrow.

"Tell me I'm wrong," Hebe said. "Tell me you put in an escape thread. Tell me you at least thought about it."

"I wasn't exactly thinking straight," said Sage.

"Jules isn't in the habit of thinking about safety either," said Viola. "We, uh…" *We always had someone around who could dismantle dangerous magic faster than either of us could construct it.*

She had an awful feeling that with Sage still too drunk to be trusted, they were going to rely on her to unwork the maze and… well, there was a reason that Viola's speciality was mythology. Unravelling magic was beyond her comfort zone, and having Chauv around had always meant that she never had to try to get over that particular weak spot. "Oh, hell. What we need is a shadowmancer."

"Hilarious," grunted Ferdinand Chauvelin, opening his eyes. "What hit me?"

"Jules," said Sage, at the same time that Mei said:

"Sage."

Chauv blinked a few times. His eyes went straight to Hebe, because of course. "Are you OK?"

"I'm worried," she said, and held out a hand to help him up.

Chauv looked to Viola next. "Where's the rogue spell I can't help you take apart because I'm not a shadowmancer any more?"

"You're standing in it," she told him.

HOLLY WAS NOT USED to being alone.

It wasn't a twin thing, okay? She and Hebe were *fine*, their issue was always needing more space from each other, not less. They weren't clingy like that.

But it felt like a really long time since Holly had seen another person. Every twist and turn of the maze dragged her deeper into isolation.

You couldn't cut the walls, or blast through them. Holly tried, once, and the damn thing all but sucked the magic out of her fingers.

There were hex traps everywhere. She had tripped twice, almost had her hand bitten off by a rogue butternut pumpkin, and narrowly avoided some very spiky straw darts.

She should have stayed where she was when the maze first hit. At least then she was only a wall away from Juniper. She hadn't been so alone.

Every now and then, the maze shook and hummed as some idiot outside tried to fix it with more magic. Those instances were getting rarer, so either the Mums and the rest of the party guests were actually listening to Juniper's warning, or they were making sensible life choices all on their own.

Or... well.

Or she was too deeply lost in this maze to even be aware of what was happening outside it.

Bad thought, Holly.

She heard a sound, not a magical sound, but a deep animal-istic growl somewhere far too close.

That... couldn't be good.

Just as she was working up a good head of panic, Holly rounded a corner and almost fell over... a throw cushion.

Unexpected.

When she looked ahead, she saw more of them, scattered liberally in a path, occasionally in-dispersed with cups of tea and plated sandwiches.

Holly had never been so grateful to see a sign of her sister's weird housewife magic in her whole life. She ran, following the trail of domestic detritus, leaping nimbly over a large teapot, and crashed smack into the large and comforting chest of her drummer. "Sage!"

"Hol!" He scooped her up and gave her a drunky hug that smelled of cider and whatever yarn his jumper was made of. "Found you."

"Found you!" she said, punching his shoulder delightedly. "Did you make this horrible place?"

"Yep."

"You're an arsehole."

"Yeh-hup."

"You're going the wrong way," said Hebe, appearing from behind the solid mass of Sage. Oh, so this was where the party was. There was Viola, May and Ferd, too. "I mean — the trail is supposed to lead us further into the maze. To collect Jules and deactivate the spell."

"That's a really optimistic view of what we're trying to achieve here," said Viola. She gave Holly that look, the 'I suspect you of never doing the readings for your tutorials' look that always marked Viola out as staff rather than student, and meant they could never 100% be friends. "How's your shadowmancy, Holly?"

"I was going to choose it as an elective," said Holly. "But it seemed hard, so I did basket-weaving instead."

Viola groaned. "This social group is cancelled."

"I always thought shadowmancy was about inventing spells," said Holly. "Don't we have enough of that going on around here?" She poked Sage in the stomach.

"Shadowmancy is about the building blocks of magic," said Ferd, his eyes brighter than usual. Everyone was always treading on eggshells around him, Holly thought, because of that whole stupid thing where he lost his magic. Probably this was the first time he'd had a chance to have a proper conversation about it in ages, which was a pity since it was clearly his favourite thing ever. "If you understand the individual components of any given spell, you can mend a faulty piece of magic or disassemble it neatly without causing any explosive fallout. But it's precision work, and it's highly reliant on a specific vocabulary to move the components around without creating more of a mess…"

"Oh," said Holly. "So like songwriting, then."

Ferd gave her a wild look. "Like *what*?"

"You know," she shrugged. "The more you understand and practice music, the more you can see where a song doesn't work. Sometimes it just takes one note to throw the whole thing off. And finding it and replacing that note — or that word — it's tricky to do. The whole thing can just collapse. That's why Sage and Juniper and I rely on each other so much to fix each other's songs when they're broken."

Ferd was staring at her like she had just reinvented caffeine-free Coke.

"What?" Holly said uncomfortably. "This can't be new information. I know you were doing that poetry course, writing spells basically the same thing…"

"Huh," said Ferd. "I can work with this."

"Work with… what?"

———

IT WASN'T SHADOWMANCY, in the end. There wasn't time for Holly to absorb an entire school of magic, not even with her 'charming lack of magical theory to unlearn' as Viola put it.

But remembering words, that much she could do. So when the group of them finally emerged to the centre of the maze, where the monstrous form of Giant Minotaur!Jules was found snacking on a wall constructed entirely from toffee apples, scorched butternut pumpkins and fun-sized Milky Way bars, Holly cast the words that Ferd had taught her. It was a three-layered revealing spell to display the charmwork Jules and Sage had come up with, in their moment of drunken creation.

"Ugh," said Viola as the words and symbols filled the air around the snacking minotaur, glowing with light. "I mean, it's brilliant. I hate that they are geniuses even when wasted. But there are words in that spell that shouldn't even exist."

"My favourite kind," Ferd said fondly.

Holly caught Viola giving her BFF a weird look like she didn't know what to do with him not being heartsick about the giant magical tragedy of his life.

But there wasn't time for any of that.

Holly and Viola took turns reading out the exposed language of the spell, which Ferd absorbed and considered before telling them which symbols to erase, which lines to cut. He couldn't see the revealed charm components at all, but he didn't seem to have lost any knowledge about how they should fit together. As they all worked, Holly felt the maze begin to fade around them, the walls thinning.

Holly was particularly pleased when she erased a whole rhyming couplet of Ancient Minoan obscenities, and Jules Nightshade promptly swooned out of the shape of a minotaur, landing shirtless on the hay-strewn ground.

"You could have caught him," Mei observed.

"My reflexes are off," said Sage, who had literally stepped out of the way to avoid catching Jules.

Mei glared at him, and waggled her comedy spectacles. "Don't sink my ship, mate. You're already on thin ice around here."

It took another twenty minutes of concentrated spell trimming before the maze cracked open like an egg, folding itself back into straw and boxes of Halloween snacks and the undamaged barn.

Holly heard a high-pitched noise, and turned around just in time to see Juniper, warm and huggable as ever, crashing into her arms. "You're okay," Juniper said happily, burying her face in Holly's neck. "I was worried."

"Nah," said Holly trying not to smile too wide. "We were having fun."

Shadowmancy, it turned out, was almost as much fun as writing songs, and she didn't want to think about *that* too hard.

Not when she had a Juniper to hug, anyway.

————

"You're good at this," Ferd said to Holly later, as they all recovered with hot mugs of chocolate and/or pumpkin soup around a dying bonfire. The Mums directed most of their protective worry at Jules and Sage, along with lectures about responsible magic use and spellcasting-under-the-influence.

It was so nice to not be the person getting those lectures. So this was what it was like to be the good sibling.

"Eh," said Holly. "I don't think I'll make a career of it."

"You should consider," said Ferd hesitantly. "I mean — The College of the Real are always looking for —"

"I graduate in six weeks," she reminded him. "I'm done with Belladonna U."

"Oh, yeah," he said in a small voice, and looked across the fire to where Hebe had joined the Mums in lecturing Sage.

"You should write us a song," Holly said impulsively. "Since shadowmancy is so close to what I do… give it a go. You might not hate it."

Ferd laughed at her, but he didn't say no. It was, hands down, the best conversation Holly had managed to share with her sister's boyfriend.

Progress had been made.

it I knew his faofts. were grieving for what he lost. But he was a
"brilliant" shadowmancer. Hal. He would have been—it's
amazing he copes as well as he does. Trying new things. I'm so
proud of him.

R0ckg0dde$$: can I see it to market?

Hebe So Boring: I'm not allowed to show it to anyone.

R0ckg0dde$$: don't mudge t .... from you.
why not mud

Hebe So Boring: I think Juniper helped him with the scansion
and then...well, I think Juniper wrote half of it, to be honest.

R0ckg0dde$$: what you're saying is that Juniper has a copy of
this poem and could se

PART THREE

EPILOGUES ARE FOR WITCHES

R0ckg0dde$$ has created this mirrorchat

R0ckg0dde$$: so Ferd wasn't trying to break up with you?

Hebe So Boring: not exactly

Hebe So Boring: he was having some kind of crisis about
everyone else graduating while he's still in undergrad. Which I
suppose puts my own graduating crisis into perspective.

R0ckg0dde$$: your shit is important too babycakes

Hebe So Boring: he wrote me a poem

R0ckg0dde$$: wow that would be an epic way to break up with
someone

Hebe So Boring: not a break up poem. It's really lovely. It's full
of — more than he ever tells me in person. About his hopes and
fears. About shadowmancy. I don't think I ever — he never
talked about it before. I didn't realise quite how good he was at

it. I knew his family were grieving for what he lost. But he was a
brilliant shadowmancer, Hol. He would have been — it's
amazing he copes as well as he does. Trying new things. I'm so
proud of him.

R0ckg0dde$$: can I set it to music?

Hebe So Boring: I'm not allowed to show it to anyone

R0ckg0dde$$: cmon Hebes I steal everything else from you,
why not this?

Hebe So Boring: I think Juniper helped him with the scansion
and the… well, I think Juniper wrote half of it, to be honest.

R0ckg0dde$$: what you're saying is that Juniper has a copy of
this poem and could secretly give me access

Hebe So Boring: don't you dare ask her!

R0ckg0dde$$: so what about Sage, are we good with Sage?

Hebe So Boring: we talked, we're… everything's good. Sorted. I
told him some things and — we're working towards being better
friends. He actually helped me figure out some my own future
shit, you know? I think I'm going to apply for Honours and work
towards getting my Masters in librarianship. There's an Unreal
Archivist program that's really exciting, about ways to preserve
books without magic. And… I'll see if they offer me a scholar-
ship. That should help the decision making process. I don't think
I'm done with uni yet.

R0ckg0dde$$: THANK YOU HOLLY FOR ENCOURAGING
OUR FRIENDZGROOP TO HAVE A LOVELY HOLIDAY
WEEKEND AND WORK THROUGH OUR EMOTIONAL
BULLSHIT TOWARDS SOME KIND OF CONSTRUCTIVE
CATHARSIS

Hebe So Boring: don't even pretend any of this was intentional on your part

R0ckg0dde$$: Oh Holly, you are my saviour, how could I possibly have survived all these years without you and the magical butternut pumpkins of stress resolution?

Hebe So Boring: pumpkins are not magic

Hebe So Boring: not even butternut pumpkins

R0ckg0dde$$: Holly you are the best twin evah, I will name my firstborn child after you and never doubt your skillz at party-planning, road trip encouraging, or Halloweening EVER EVAH AGAIN.

Hebe So Boring: Holly

Hebe So Boring: Halloween is not a verb

Hebe So Boring: and I admit nothing

Hebe So Boring: but thanks :*

R0ckg0dde$$: *[custom butternut pumpkin poledancing dancemoji]*

R0ckg0dde$$: *[custom minotaur doing the macarena dancemoji]*

R0ckg0dde$$: *[smugface smugface smugface, bootyshake dancemoji, scarecrow, jack o'lantern, smugface]*

SOLSTICE ON THE ROCKS

CHAPTER ONE
GRADUATION

HEBE

HOLLY'S HAIR is fire engine red. Red like a bag of Jaffas. It looks fierce over her black graduation gown. Mine is the same shade of red, because she insisted we be identical today. It doesn't suit me nearly so well. I can't carry off bold.

(Somehow, Holly pulled together enough credits to graduate at the same time as me, despite half-arsing her degree for the last three years. It's infuriating, and yet… OMG I would have been so mad at her if we didn't get to do this together.)

Today is the Summer Solstice. By rights we should be home already, drinking mint-flavoured booze and taking part in all kinds of arcane rituals involving fresh cherries, cold prawns and desserts that are better suited to Midwinter (because, as always, Australian witches live in an upside down world). It's also the last day of Graduation Week.

Sage had his ceremony yesterday. Dec's done too, and Juniper and Mei. Just me and Holly to go.

The Mums are here, snapping pictures and hugging each other.

It all feels so very, very final.

It's not. Not for me. I'm either continuing here in Honours next year, or… well, I'm still waiting to hear if I got in to the magical archivists diploma course that I'm dying to do, even if it does mean stepping over the divide into the College of the Real. I'm not done with Belladonna University, not by a long shot.

But it feels done. Like this is the last time we'll all see each other. (It's ridiculous, most of us share a house)

I can't stop hugging people.

I don't know where Ferd's got to. He was supposed to be here, for the ceremony. Not just for me, but for Jules. He hasn't answered any of my texts. This isn't like him.

———

JUNIPER

Jules Nightshade is having a panic attack behind the Unreal Arts Building, and I'm the only witness.

We're not exactly friends. So many friends in common, but we've rarely shared a conversation. Deep down, I know that he's the sort of boy who would have mocked my cello at primary school, or laughed along with my sisters when they pranked me. He's not a nice person.

But Viola and Ferd adore him. Sage keeps gravitating back to him like he's a Darcy and not an obvious scoundrel of a Wickham. (Sage himself is more of a Knightley, or maybe a Colonel Brandon... but I'm getting distracted.)

It doesn't matter what Jules is. He could be the worst of Willoughbies and I'd still want to help him through this time of trouble. I don't know him very well, but I know panic attacks.

He's crouching low against the wall, fighting for breath. I lament the risk to my long hand-made patchwork skirt to kneel in front of him. "Jules. Count your breaths slowly. Can you do that?"

He stares at me, barely seeing me, completely disoriented.

"I'm going to take your hands." One after the other, I take his clammy hands in mine. He's wearing a suit under his graduation robe, and I'm pretty sure it cost more than my year's tuition debt. "Count your breaths. Get to five."

He does that, with difficulty.

"Tell me something you can feel, something you can see, something you can hear," I command, pulling out a half-remembered technique that used to help me when I was on the floor about exams in school.

"Gravel path," he manages. "Your nightmare of a skirt." Rude. "Orchestra?"

"It's the school's back up orchestra," I tell him. "They're terrible. Especially the second flautist. Who was also mean about my skirt today, actually. You'd probably get on."

He laughs shakily, back with me. Embarrassment is starting to flood across his cheeks as he settles back into his surroundings. "Thanks. You didn't have to help."

How little he knows me. "Always here to aid a gentleman in distress. Are you okay now?"

"Fine." Nightshade is putting his armour back on, all posture and elegance, though he's clearly a long way from 'fine'. I watch him rise to his feet, then extend a hand to help me up. "Don't tell anyone. Please."

"Of course I won't."

Does this mean we're friends now? How very confusing.

VIOLA

Viola is seething with anger. It flickers through her veins, makes her nails itch. She wants to set fire to the university's flapping banner overhead.

It's a hot day, all sharp sunshine and thick air. Viola hates it. How has she never got around to reviving the parasol trend? Instead she stands in giant sunglasses and a wide-brimmed hat, exchanging social chit-chat with Irene Nightshade as they wait for Jules to rejoin them. He's been looking pale all morning, as the ceremony draws closer.

That's what he gets for winning two of the university's most prestigious Real Prizes for the year. (Sage, of course, won three, and delivered a blinder of a speech yesterday, all broad humour and self-deprecation)

Chauv hasn't turned up, which is an utter betrayal, and not even close to the top of the list of what is pissing Viola off right now.

Speaking of Sage, there he is — wearing a buttoned shirt, of all things. Not even flannel. Yesterday, at his own ceremony, he wore a new Kraken tee underneath his robes, and Viola is convinced he skipped the trousers all together for board shorts. Today, he's pretending to be respectable, of course, for Hebe's sake — or, more to the point, for Hebe's three adorable mothers who are all in attendance.

"Vale," Sage greets her as he yobs past, making Irene Nightshade stiffen in alarm like she's in danger of being mugged. "Seen Juniper?"

"Not recently," says Viola, smiling sweetly. That should have been his warning to run like hell. "Let me introduce you to Irene. Jules' mother," she adds.

To his credit, Sage barely flinches at meeting the glamorous mother of the bloke he's been shagging on and off for most of the year. "Nice to meet you, Irene. You must be proud of him."

"Yes," said Irene, looking startled. "Extremely proud."

There's Jules, finally, making his way through the crowd with Juniper of all people trotting along at his side.

"Mother," he says, his very presence cooling everyone down a degree or two, like he has arrived with a tray of iced tea. "Shall we go in?"

"I was just meeting your friend, dear," says Irene, drawing her hand back from Sage with a polite smile. "And who is —"

Viola introduces Juniper, since that is apparently her role in today's events. Making other people mildly uncomfortable helps to settle the burning rage in her heart, so. Why not be a hostess?

"Irene," blurts Juniper as she grasps the pallid hand of Jules' mother and shakes it a little too enthusiastically. "That's the same name as my cello."

"Charmed," says Irene.

"Let's go in," says Jules wildly. He looks like he's been

snorting something expensive behind the bins, but Viola chooses to take pity on him. She conjures a comb between her fingers, and tidies his hair. "You're going to be great," she tells him sternly, so he has no other choice but to be great.

At least it's an indoors ceremony. She won't have to endure the sickening heat for too long.

Jules scoffs at her. "Obviously. Be ready to catch my mother when she swoons over my brilliance."

Sage barks out a sudden laugh at that, and their eyes graze each other.

Give me strength, Viola thinks impatiently. Still, she can't prevent a wave of affection and nostalgia from overtaking her in their presence.

There's no sign of Jules' dad, or of Chauvelin. Only one of these absences is a disappointment; no one ever gained anything from expecting Mr West Nightshade to make good choices.

"Break a leg!" yelps Juniper.

Jules gives her a weirdly fond sort of smile. "You're such a mean girl," he assures her, as if it's the greatest compliment he could bestow.

What the hell. Are they friends now? How do these things keep happening?

CHAPTER TWO
ART

SAGE

ART GALLERIES ARE NOT my cup of tea, or my half-glass of cab
sav some arsehole ordered in bulk because of its wanky hipster
label with a shoe on it.

But Dec's a mate. When your mate has his first proper art
exhibition in Real Life After Uni, you turn up. (Even if uni only
finished like, five minutes ago)

We're putting on a good show of it, all dolled up from Hebe
and Hol's (and Jules') graduation, the last day of ceremonies.

Turns out, we're way over-dressed. Dec's previous show, the
one he did for school about six weeks ago, was all wineglasses
and snooty professors in a bright white square of a gallery. This
one, meanwhile, is in a hole-in-the-wall corner of a converted
factory in a corner of the city so dodgy that we couldn't get an
Uber to bring us here.

Drinks are served from jam jars, and the music is electro-
punk playing out of someone's old car stereo. Paint-spattered
mannequins hang from the ceiling. You must be *this* tattooed to
enter.

Way more cool than I'd expected. "Didn't Vale use her
connections to sign Dec up for some kind of fancy pants gallery

in the hotel district?" I ask Jules in a low voice when I finally
drag him away from his phone.

"He turned it down," says Jules with a mocking shrug.
"Didn't like the corporate vibe. I guess he's not planning to be
one of those artists who earns money?"

Behind us, an old lady with bright pink hair slaps down three
hundreds into a shoebox so she can put a red sticker on what I
thought was a cheese platter made from a chipped vinyl record.

"Guess not," I say absently. Where the hell's Dec, anyway?
If his mates have to stand around drinking out of jam jars, he
should be here to laugh at us.

Jules has recovered fiercely from whatever the hell was
going on with him earlier. He's blazing ice-cold like a beacon,
all smouldering flirtation and 'I know how to hold a jam jar like
it's a wine glass.' It's obscenely attractive. I don't deserve this.

We're crammed between Dec's Maenad sculpture and a
lamp-post with plastic doll heads dangling from it. Hebe and
Holly are standing on the other side of the lamp-post — they've
got the same hair for the first time in years, a punch-you-in-the-
face shiny red colour that is going to be a fun surprise for Ferd
when he finally shows up. (Nothing like accidentally groping
your girlfriend's sister, a mistake I only made about three times
at high school before Holly cracked out baby's first home dye
packet.)

Hol is hyped as hell, working her way down her second jar
of cheap wine. She I vibrating with a near constant hum that
sounds a lot like the work 'karaoke' because yeah, it's a
Thursday night, no escaping that.

"I'm not singing," I warn her as I make a break for what is
either an actual platter of cheese on toothpicks, or an ironic $300
exhibit that I definitely shouldn't touch.

"Oh," says Holly, swishing her bright red hair around like
she hopes to set fire to someone with it. "You're singing, mate."

VIOLA

It's not the first time that Viola and Dec have fucked in a storage cupboard full of stacked-up artworks and cleaning supplies. Somehow, when you're dating an artist, cardboard boxes and piles of canvases become the white noise background of your life.

There's a frenetic heat to this particular fuck, though, which has been missing from their relationship lately. Dec has gone from intense work on his final exhibition for uni to this, his first 'grown up' show. And Viola... well, Viola keeps screwing up.

Getting her father to arrange that other gallery offer, the one that would lead to her boyfriend's successful future, that was the first big screwup. First of many. Last of many?

Dec wasn't even pissed off about it, he shrugged it off like it was nothing, like the whole thing was confusing and pointless. (Like he had no idea what it cost her to ask her father for anything, which is fair actually because... they've never had that conversation. There's a lot of conversations they've never had.)

Dec doesn't get it. When she pushed (another screwup), poking and prodding enough to get Dec actually to state an opinion, he finally said to her: *what kind of artist do you think I am*?

(What he didn't say was: what kind of artist boyfriend did you think you were getting? But she heard it, in his tone.)

She loves that he made art of her.

But yeah. They don't exactly fit right now.

They keep missing each other. They fight more than they should (Dec hates fighting, she knows that, and somehow she keeps manipulating him to the point that they're both yelling at each other, because that makes sense to her in a way that literally nothing else about their relationship ever has).

Viola hates that this is probably the last time they are going to have sex, and she is so stressed and on edge that she probably isn't even going to —

Oh, damn, that's good. How is this so good?

It's infuriating: even when everything else is falling apart, they are still so good at this.

Viola braces herself against a countertop stacked with boxes, legs up and around his waist. She loves the feeling of Dec inside her, of the weight of his body. She is going to — miss…

(She digs her fingernails into the back of his neck when she comes, wanting to leave a mark.)

"We don't have to break up," he says, minutes later, still catching his breath.

"That's not what you said this morning," snaps Viola, checking her lipstick.

She can still feel the marks from the boxes where they dug into the back of her thighs. She should probably get a tetanus shot.

"I was pissed off this morning," says Dec, running his fingers through his hair. He looks sad, which is worse than fighting. "I didn't mean it."

Viola sighs. "I'm pissed off *now*. And I mean everything I say, always. So what are we going to do about that?"

HEBE

Ferd isn't here. Holly's nervous about something. She's bouncing around this room making friends like it's going out of style. I still haven't wrapped my head around how she demanded we look the same today, something she hasn't wanted since we were fifteen.

I'm a graduated person. I don't feel any different, except that this morning I knew where my boyfriend was going to be today, and now I have no idea why he's not returning my texts.

It sucks that I'm hanging around waiting for him. Except… I'm not waiting. I'm drinking awful wine with Mei and trying to convince her to come with me to Holly's karaoke thing.

"Nope nope nope, you get one graduation wish," she says, eyes on Mirrorweb instead of me. "You get an epic D&D campaign, which Dec and I have been preparing for weeks. It starts at midnight. Don't be late."

"I didn't wish for that," I grumble, though I'm secretly delighted. A Mei and Dec one-shot is a rare honour. Last time, they made special hats and shirts.

"We wished it for you," says Mei. "You're welcome." She lifts her jam jar of cheap wine and stares at it dubiously. "Are you going to buy any art?"

"Out of my price range."

I'm probably going to be a student for another year. Three jobs with not enough hours in any of them, city rent that's a grind to pay despite sharing with so many people. Real life can't start yet.

"I'm going to buy some art," Mei decides, and heads for a display of plastic mannequins with forks impaled in their flat, bland stomachs.

"Did I mention I *really* don't want any Solstice gifts this year?" I call after her.

My phone buzzes, but it's not Ferd. It's the Mums in our group chat, suggesting I come home for a while, once we're done with our celebrating. Bring my boyfriend if he's free. Do the Solstice properly.

It's not like I have any other plans between now and New Year's Eve.

I don't know where my boyfriend is, so I guess I can't ask him.

This wine tastes like the jar was previously used for turpentine.

I'm done.

Holly blitzes past me on the arm of a celebrity music journo. Trust her to find the most famous person in the room. "Karaoooooooke," she carols, bopping her head.

Ugh, yes. That.

CHAPTER THREE
KARAOKE

TEXTS TO FERD

HOLLY: dude where R you? Karaoke night at Medea's C don be late

JULES: wtf where were you today? Mum says your sister's in town. Are you doing family shit? Finally? We would have come with you.

VIOLA: Call me, Chauv. I need to talk to someone.

HEBE: Is everything all right? This isn't like you.

SAGE: Mate. Seriously? What the fuck.

DEC: Hebe's like five minutes away from calling all the hospitals. In case you were wondering.

JUNIPER: Dear Ferdinand. I hope you are well. Please let us know where you are, as Hebe seems rather concerned. Best regards, Juniper Cresswell.

HOLLY: karaoke or bust, dickhead - B there
or else

SAGE

JUNIPER AND JULES are singing My Familiar together because
apparently they levelled up to karaoke duet friends when I
wasn't looking. Not the weirdest thing that's happened tonight,
but pretty fucken weird.

Holly's mission is to get me to pick a karaoke song but until
Kraken (or Fake Geek Girl!) get on the automated rotation, you
can leave me out of this group activity. I've got beer to swallow,
and boys to leer at.

Jules looks good on stage. He can't sing for shit, but he could
probably strum a bass guitar if he had to. His hair is bright under
the dodgy spotlight. He looks like he's having fun.

I need to not take him home tonight. No matter how tight
those jeans fit him. And I swear, they're getting tighter.

"Sage," says a voice, and I swing around to — damn. Last
person I wanna see, maybe. Evan, the goth barista from Cirque
De Cacao, out of his natural environment. (Definitely Evan, not
Will, I have memorised the damned piercings this time.) He
looks good.

"Hey," I say, because this is awkward.

"Can we talk?" he asks.

Shit.

"I'm kind of in the middle of…" Literally nothing. "Sure."

Vale hip-checks me as we walk past her. She sways, looking
way too drunk for this early in the evening, even with karaoke in
the mix.

"Hey," I say, steadying her with a hand. "You all right?"

"Avalon," she says, and pats my cheek. "Don't forget."

HEBE

"We're singing together," says Holly, shoving a tablet at me so I can scroll through the song choices.

"I'm really not in the mood," I warn her.

"We are going to celebrate graduation if it kills you."

"Oh, well, as long as it kills me."

Juniper joins us at the booth, pink-faced and pleased with herself. "That's my brave thing ticked off for the month," she informs us.

Holly rolls her eyes. "We performed a live gig at this bar three weeks ago."

"Karaoke is way scarier," Juniper insists.

"No cello to hide behind," Holly teases.

Without Mei and Dec here, I'm officially the least sociable person at the pub. I pull out my phone to stare at it, just in case Ferd's texted me back, but Holly flicks it out of my hand. "No, no more pining. Your arsehole boyfriend can meet us at Avalon."

"What's Avalon?" asks Juniper, as if her entire role in life is to feed Holly straight lines. (Wow, I'm catty tonight, I should cut myself off from… everything.)

Holly's eyes light up. "You wait."

"It's a club," I sigh.

"Not just any club. It's a secret club that moves around the city. You need the password to get in, and even then it's almost impossible to find."

"That sounds stressful," says Juniper brightly.

"But tonight we have a secret weapon!" insists Holly. "Viola knows someone who knows someone."

"Oh, with impeccable credentials like that…" I murmur. My feet are hurting, even sitting down. I want to get out of here and go roll dice with Dec and Mei. But Holly has her hooks into me, and if I go home now, there will be no one to stop me looking at my phone.

"Who does Viola know?" interrupts Jules, coming over with a giant jug of margarita, and a tray full of glasses. "Has that minx been making other friends?"

"She didn't say, but she can totally get us in," says Holly, bouncing. "*Avalon.*"

"If it doesn't have hot boys in wet shirts handing out swords, I don't care," says Jules, peering through the messy crowd. "There she is."

Viola is standing in the corner, talking to a stupidly handsome bloke in a suit far too fancy for the pub. He looks vaguely familiar, though I can't put my finger on why.

Then a second man joins them, and I choke on a mouthful of frozen tequila and lime. "*No.*" Campion bloody Merryweather. Of course he's one of that Basilisk crowd. I can't think why it didn't occur to me before, that Ferd and Jules would know him. He's been blissfully out of our lives for nearly a year now, since he and Holly split for what I desperately hope was the final time.

Jules and Holly see him at the same time and exchange a mutual "Ugh," then give each other a suspicious look.

"Wait," says Jules. "Why?"

"Ex," says Holly with narrowed eyes. "You?"

"I choose not to answer that question on the grounds that I might incriminate myself."

She rolls her eyes, and clinks glasses with him, "Cheers, sweetie."

"So no Avalon?" I ask hopefully.

Holly gives me a furious expression. I might have known. "Yes, Avalon."

A figure all in black swings into view. I blink, and Will, one of the goth baristas from Cirque De Cacao, comes into focus. "Have you seen Sage and my brother?" he demands, with an air of pent-up fury.

"*Cheers,*" says Jules brightly, and clinks his glass to mine.

CHAPTER FOUR
AVALON

JUNIPER

I'M NOT beautiful enough for Avalon, but somehow we're here anyway. Viola is trailing around a new entourage consisting of Holly's nightmare ex-boyfriend Campion, and his brother whom everyone seems to be referring to as The Good Merryweather.

Sage is in a terribly bad mood, and has acquired a gentleman friend with several interesting piercings.

Jules abandoned us all the second we got here, claiming to be on the hunt for 'strange boys lying in ponds distributing swords as a system of government' which I think might be a euphemism for something. Best not to ask too many questions.

Holly hasn't left my side. She was so excited about this club, but now Campion is here, she is far more interested in hiding out in corners and pretending that everything Hebe and I say is hilarious.

Everyone in this club is so pretty, it's exhausting.

HEBE

Just another booth in another place serving over-priced booze, and I can't even check my phone because Holly confiscated it.

"I texted him we were coming here," she informs me. "And I bet you did the same. But you know…"

Yeah, I know. It's late, and I haven't heard from Ferd all day. I have officially been blown off.

What's the time window for being ghosted? Ignored for one day, that's easy enough to explain if a phone was lost or ran out of charge. Even a really important day. At what point do I stop worrying he's been in an accident and start worrying that he just doesn't want to talk to me?

"I've stopped thinking about him," I lie.

"Sure," says Holly, "But can you stop thinking about him while also pretending that we're having an amazing time?" She eyes her ex across the room and smiles a wide, carefully careless smile.

"I can do that," I agree, and make myself look happy, for her sake.

It's graduation, after all.

————

SAGE

We made it to Avalon, big whoop. One of those clubs that's way more fun to wonder about, than to actually spend time in.

Everything is moon white: the walls, the glowing light orbs that illuminated the spherical room (veins of purple crackle across the light orbs every now and then, throwing out an unhealthy glow that makes everyone look dead). The servers, in crisp white aprons and fairy wingspan hand out spiked bubble tea and slushies from tall white cups, over a long, thick glass bar that's clearly an accident waiting to happen.

Everything feels breakable.

Vale is dancing with Campion Merryweather, like she has

something to prove. Don't know who she's proving it to, since Dec and Mei went home hours ago. To play board games, I think? Reckon I should have gone with them.

Evan has found some mates, which is a relief because we've run out of things to talk about. I ease away from him and his crowd with the promise of bringing back a drink.

Jules appears out of nowhere as I lean over the glass bar. Somehow, in the twenty minutes since we got here, he has managed to completely cover himself in glitter. The harsh white light that brings out the worst in the rest of us makes him glow like a sprite.

"Having fun?" he drawls.

"It's the best." I glance behind me, to where Viola has moved on to the other Merryweather brother, the one who doesn't make my teeth ache. "So which of us is making sure she gets home okay?"

"I'll handle it," Jules promises. "No one here worth going home with, and you seem to have got yourself married when I wasn't looking…"

"Ha ha." I wonder what kind of face the server will pull if I order a beer. It's almost worth it.

"So one of your latest pair of twins forgave you?" he adds with his usual annoying brand of 'getting to the point so hard it stabs you in the face.'

"*Yup*."

"Is this Evan or Will?"

"Evan. Will's still pissed off at me. At both of us, now."

Jules smirks. "You like Will better than Evan, don't you?"

"Shut *up*." How does he know these things?

He spins on the stool with a flourish. "Dance with me? Make them both jealous?"

"Will's not even here," I grumble.

"Offer stands." He holds out his hand to me.

Dancing would be a great way to admit to everyone in this whole stupid club that I'd rather be dancing with Jules than Will or Evan or literally anyone else.

"Yeah, nah, better not."

"Your loss," Jules says lightly, like it cost him nothing to ask, or to be turned down. He spins off into the night, shiny and beautiful.

So that's a thing that happened tonight.

—————

JUNIPER

"Kenneth's here," says Hebe, staring at her drink because none of us will allow her to stare at her phone.

"Who?" says Holly, not paying attention.

Hebe blinks. "Your current boyfriend? He's over by the bar."

"Oh, him." Holly shrugs. "He can see me anytime. This is sister time."

"That's sweet," says Hebe. "But you don't have to…"

Holly doesn't even glance in Kenneth's direction, too busy darting secretive looks over to where Viola and her pair of Merryweathers are partying hard. Other have joined them now, beautiful warlock children in designer outfits. Her old crowd, I suppose.

Viola and Jules and Chauvelin must have other friends, but for most of last year, they've never mentioned any of them. They've lived in our pockets, hanging out with the band, crashing every weekend in at the Manic Pixie Dream House.

Is that over now, if Viola isn't with Dec, and Ferd is… whatever Ferd is doing? Now that most of us have graduated. Do we just stop hanging out?

Sage and Holly haven't said a word about the fact that we only have one more gig to play at Medea's Cauldron, in January, and then that's it. We're not a Belladonna U band anymore. We'll have to grow up, find another venue, or…

Seriously. Not one word. It's almost as if they both forgot that graduation means everything changes.

"He's coming over," sighs Hebe, without looking. Does her magic actually alert her to the activities of Holly's terrible boyfriends? That would be terrible useful, really.

"Which one?" asks Holly, grinning manically at me so as not to look in either direction.

"Um," says Hebe.

So, both, then.

"Holly Hallow, long time no see," drawls Campion Merryweather, his hand latched around Viola's wrist. She looks annoyed, and drunk, but mostly annoyed.

"Holly, babe, didn't know you were gonna be here," says Kenneth, sliding into the booth without being invited. He gives me a Look until I budge up to make room. (There is no more room.)

"Viola," says Hebe, ignoring everyone else. "Have you heard from —?"

"I would have told you," says Viola, biting out the words like she had a grudge against them. Her ice-white cocktail is down to the dregs. "He hasn't texted me all day."

I feel hot and trapped with this many people crowded around the booth. I have never wanted to get out of somewhere so much in all my life.

(Which is saying something, really.)

To top it all off, there's an awkward pause, which probably only lasts a few seconds. To me, it's an eternity. It ends when I actually see the genuine article, Ferdinand Chauvelin himself, walk into view across the other side of the blinding white club.

He's wearing a peacock blue silk shirt over grey trousers, and while I've seen him dressed up fancy enough in recent months, I haven't seen him look like that before. He oozes Rich Snobby Person Who Will Give You The Cut Direct. He doesn't look like the kind of person who would ever be friends with me, or Mei, or Hebe.

"Oh look!" I say in a terribly bright tone of voice. "There he is."

Everyone turns to look.

Hebe's drink glass transforms itself into a teacup, a hiccup of her magic under stress.

"Mystery solved!" declares Viola with a dramatic wave of her glass.

"Not really," says Hebe, sounding very quiet. Slowly, she clambers out of the booth (climbing over Holly to do it) and makes her way towards her stray boyfriend.

Sage appears behind our booth holding what looks like an actual beer. "Hey," he says, looking rather hunted. "Anyone want to go back to ours for board games?"

Campion Merryweather snorts in derision, as does the terrible Kenneth.

"But Avalon," protests Holly weakly. Agreeing to leave would put paid to her illusion of having a wonderful time.

Miss Juniper Cresswell, meanwhile, has never been so happy to see Sage in her entire life. "*Yes,*" I gasp with great enthusiasm. "Let's go."

CHAPTER FIVE
AFTER PARTY

SAGE

IT'S bad that I ditched Evan, yeah? He was angling to come back with us and I just couldn't even pretend that I wanted that.

I claimed there was some friendship drama going on I had to sort, which was probably gonna be true by the end of the night, but it still made me feel shitty because we both knew it was an excuse.

The rest of us walked back to the house in twos and threes, an aimless parade through the streets, too tired to make conversation that made sense.

I hung back, and still ended up walking with Jules. Honestly. I didn't mean to. Some nights just put you in the right place at the right time. (The wrong place, the wrong time.)

"I had a panic attack today," he blurted out, staring at the pavement as we shambled along.

I glanced around— everyone else was far ahead or in front of us. No one to hear. Juniper, who had been hovering around Jules all night, was marching far up front like she was leading us on a Scouting hike up a mountain.

"You all right?" I asked in a low voice.

"Yeah. I feel stupid."

"Nothing new there."

Jules bumped into me deliberately and laughed. "Cheers."

"No worries. Something on your mind?"

"It's going to make me sound like a wanker."

"When has that ever stopped you?"

He laughed again but sounded uneasy now. "It's just — uni's over. Like, *over*."

"Changed your mind about sticking around for postgrad?"

"Hell, no. It's just — I never had to try that hard, you know."

One of the many things that was irritating about Jules Nightshade. At least he knew it.

"I'm aware." I'd done my fair share of slacking off. When you have a lot of power, it's easy to get complacent. But I never took my education for granted — whenever I caught myself skipping classes or dashing off a last minute prac report, I'd remember how lucky I was to go to a place like Belladonna U. How hard my family fought to deny me that chance.

Jules didn't have anything like that. He had more natural talent and control than me, too, though I could blow him out of the water with raw power.

"Uni's over for me," Jules went on, like his problem should be obvious. "I was a Basilisk King, man. No matter what class I took, the professors already knew I was tenth generation warlock, that my family had endowed buildings. My parents and grandfather are both active on the Board... Anything I wanted, I got."

"It's hard to like you sometimes."

"I had a gold-plated fucking safety net."

"And you're complaining?"

"No, just — starting to wonder what it's going to be like, giving all that up. Starting work in a company where my family don't own everything I touch. Can I hack it? Am I any good? Maybe I was never any good." He was starting to twitch.

I settled him with an arm slung across his shoulders. Not making a move. Just pressing him down. "Jules. Mate. You are actually as talented as professors think you are, you know. That's why you piss people off."

"Yeah?" he asked, in a small voice.

"You know this. Also, what the hell. You do know that wealth, privilege and family contacts are still very much in play outside uni, right?"

I could see him relaxing, damn it. The last thing he needed was ego stroking, especially when I was determined there wasn't going to be any of the fun kind of stroking between him and me, not any more.

"That's true," Jules said slowly.

"Believe me, you're gonna be fine. Easiest fucken setting for life. If you're worried you won't be brilliant enough on your first day? Make more of an effort. But don't like, knock yourself out. Ten percent of Jules Nightshade brilliance is more than enough for anyone."

He leaned his head against the side of my neck. His hair smelled amazing. "Is that really what you think?"

"Have you ever known me to be nice to you on purpose?"

"Sure," he said, dragging the word out. "Yeah, you're such hard case, McClaren. Not a marshmallow at all."

Damn it. He's on to me.

———

HEBE

There are two after parties. One happening upstairs, with Holly juggling two men she doesn't care about, Viola acting like she's having the time of her life, and Sage pretending he doesn't want to eat Jules alive. I spent five minutes at that party, and I wanted to beat myself unconscious with a broomstick.

Then there's the real party, with me and Mei and Juniper and Dec, hanging out in the living room downstairs, sitting around a coffee table covered with miniatures of orcs and wizards and dragons.

I broke up with my boyfriend an hour ago, and I haven't told anyone. I don't intend to tell anyone. Let Ferd break it to our roommates. I'm heading home to the Mums tomorrow to drown my sorrows in wholesome Solstice celebrations with the Hallow clan.

I don't want anyone taking sides. I don't want to talk it through with my well-meaning friends and sister. I don't want anyone trying to cheer me up, or make me feel better. Right now, I just want to slay some monsters.

Dec is wearing his Dungeon Master's hat, which means this is serious. "Nevermore Castle has been let at last," he intones. "According to village gossip, the new tenant is a very wealthy, unmarried vampire and his equally wealthy, eligible friends."

"I may swoon," Juniper whispers.

"Are you freaking kidding me?" I mutter.

"You are a party of impoverished orcs, wizards and dragon shifters, recently graduated from Adventure Academy. To fund your next quest, at least one of you has to marry well. You have been invited to a ball at Nevermore Castle. What do you do?"

"Take all my swords to the blacksmith for sharpening, and discreetly inquire whether there are any bounties on the heads of the new vampires in town," says Mei, who will always choose assassination over romance no matter what the specs of the game. I love her so much.

"Head to the dressmakers to find out what vampire fashions are achievable on a minimal budget!" says Juniper.

I huff a sigh, because I really don't want a romance game right now. "Check for traps," I say sourly.

Dec looks the most cheerful I've seen him all day. All week, maybe. "On the invitation?"

"*Everywhere.*"

He winks at me and I try not to smile in response. "Good call, Hebes."

Sage and Jules arrive with a carton of beer and a pizza from upstairs. "Not too late to join in?" Sage whines.

Juniper looks suspicious, but gives in faster than I might have expected. "Jules is not allowed to make fun of us."

"Miss Cresswell," said Jules, sounding shocked. "As if I would!" He squeezes in next to her on the floor. "Can I be a pretty pretty wood elf?"

"You can be an angry war dwarf, or a narcoleptic dragon," says Dec. Of course he has extra character sheets ready.

"Dragon!" says Jules, with grabby hands.

"Dwarf me, mate," says Sage, squishing in on the other side of me and reading through his character sheet. "You okay over there, Hebes?"

"I'm fine," I tell him impatiently. "Roll the dice. Let's play."

KISSING BASILISKS

CHAPTER ONE
FERD DOESN'T HAVE MAGIC

ON NEW YEAR'S DAY, Ferdinand Chauvelin woke up in a bed that wasn't his own or his girlfriend's. This was not out of character for him at 18 (when he had no girlfriend and no concept of 'time to stop drinking, mate,') but very much out of character for him now, at 21.

"Why?" he groaned when the first thing he saw was Dec's squashed-pillow face sticking out from under the blankets.

His flatmate grunted. "You gave Jules and Vi your bed to keep Jules from climbing in with Sage. Juniper's sharing with Hebe downstairs. Mei went to bed early and refused to share with anyone. Holly has her fella." Even half asleep, Dec rolled his eyes at that one. Everyone hated Holly's new fella.

Ferd sat up slowly. He felt rough, not just from whatever the hell they had been drinking last night. His whole body felt strange, like it didn't entirely belong to him. His feet pricked with pins and needles. He opened his mouth to ask why Jules hadn't bunked in with him, so Dec at least could share with his girlfriend, but something stirred in his memory: that was a bad question to ask. Right. Figure that part out later.

"How do you even remember where everyone ended up?" he muttered instead.

"Chart on the fridge," said Dec, his sentence trailing off into a snore.

Right. Good.

Ferd climbed out of bed. Someone had to put on the coffee. They usually relied on Dec for that, but he didn't look like he was gonna pull his usual Suzy Sunshine early morning bullshit right now.

Ferd was wearing boxers and an over-sized Fake Geek Girl t-shirt he must have raided from the never-ending stash of band merch. It would do. He headed out to the kitchen. The lino was cold under his bare feet, but it was supposed to get stupid hot this weekend, right? The little house they shared as two flats with the girls downstairs had terrible insulation which meant freezing mornings even in summer, and fuck-off heat from lunchtime through to about ten in the evening.

No bushfires yet near the city, which already made this a better New Year than the last one.

(Other things that sucked about last New Year included the fact that he was still living home then, and had to attend some stupid rich warlock party where his parents' friends watched him with veiled pity from behind their designer cocktails.)

Now, as the cold seeped into his feet, and the coffee pot warmed on the stove (because he was so useless he couldn't use magic to heat water any more), Ferd contemplated his messy memories from the night before.

Sangria. He remembered sangria, and oranges injected with vodka, and a bunch of other catering choices that seemed like a bloody wonderful idea yesterday.

His mouth tasted like old cloves and dead animal. Possibly floor.

The water from the tap ran cold, and he chugged half a glass of it down, thinking over what he could remember.

Viola and Dec had some kind of awful fight that started before the party with quiet jabs at each other, and built up over the evening with bursts of shouting, in-dispersed with ignoring each other, making out with other people, and throwing vodka oranges. So. That was a big awkward question that he should probably never ask either of them. Sounded like their break up was sticking… or the not-break-up was failing. One of the two, for definite.

Ferd turned around, pressing his face to the cold of the fridge because now he was remembering something else about last night. Something awful. Something world-destroying.

Shit.

Shit.

Shit.

He kissed Jules Nightshade.

No, Jules had kissed him.

Either way, Ferd now knew what it was like to have his best friend's tongue in his mouth, without any kind of drunken party game excuse.

That was.

Yeah.

Had he told Hebe yet? Did she know? Had he confessed all, knowing she might be understandably freaked out that her second serious boyfriend in her whole life was also gay?

Nah, he wasn't gay.

He definitely shouldn't have been kissing Jules, though.

Maybe Hebe knew all about it. Maybe that was why she had Juniper in with her, and why Ferd had been banished to the right side of Dec's bed.

Shit.

Ferd had been carefully ignoring Jules Nightshade's crush on him for years now. He'd been good at ignoring it. What the hell happened to change that? What kind of self-destructive idiot was he?

At least there was coffee.

The one benefit of losing all his magic in the worst accident in Belladonna University's history, fifteen months ago, was that Ferd could drink delicious, wakey-uppy liquid caffeine any time of the day without worrying it was going to affect his powers.

Well, that and his girlfriend, the literal greatest thing that had ever happened to him. He wouldn't have met Hebe without losing his magic. He wouldn't be living here with Dec and Sage, hanging out with their rock band and associated friends.

He wouldn't be studying the political significance of magical integration in Australia, which was surprisingly interesting.

He would have a degree in shadowmancy by now, planning for his career in Grey Ops. Probably sifting through job offers from a list of elite families who all wanted to curry favour with his father: High Warlock of the Basilisk Board and respectedmember of several other high status Boards around the city.

Ferd might even be engaged to Viola Vale (assuming they both eventually caved to the pressure from their parents, for want of better offers, or made a pact to humour the olds long enough to get some great presents out of the deal). He might be dressing more like his father in public. Maybe he wouldn't have figured out yet that his old life was slowly choking the oxygen out of him.

He would definitely not have let his guard down long enough to make out with his best friend, or allow himself to be made out with.

A wave of dizziness pulsed through Ferd, and he pushed away from the fridge. Wow. This was the weirdest hangover he'd had in a...

There was a handprint. A shadow of a handprint, outlined on the fridge, overlapping the actual goddamned chart of who slept where last night (he had assumed Dec was kidding), and the cool white surface.

Ferd leaned in and prodded at the shadow hand. It rippled, and a corresponding sensation tugged at his stomach.

Oh.

Oh, he was an idiot.

He hadn't been drinking last night, not after the first mouthful of sangria. (So, he had literally no excuse for what had happened with Jules, but that was a thought to unpack later.)

He wasn't hungover.

This feeling — the numbness and slowness, the sluggish haze swamping his brain. Ferd knew this feeling. He felt it when he woke up from the coma, after the lab accident that wrecked his old life. He felt it when he was a stupid kid whose magic wasn't under control yet, when he was a teenager who left scorch marks on the ceiling every time he got hard.

This familiar grinding ache in his muscles, *this* was how he felt after pulling three all-nighters in a row during First Year, trying to finish up the shadowmancy project that scored him a top mentor in the department, the project that marked him out as a Great Talent.

The project that almost killed him when he returned to it later, because he never learned his fucking limits.

Ferd reached out and touched the shadow mark on the fridge, the outline of his hand. It rippled and closed slowly around his fist, like a glove that wanted to eat him alive.

He ran to the bathroom and threw up, noisily and wetly, into the toilet. His stomach felt like it was on fire and full of concrete at the same time.

When he was done, he stuck his whole head under the shower for one quick burst of cold water, rinsing off his face and the inside of his mouth. Then, wet and shivering like an idiot, he pulled off the t-shirt and stared at himself in the mirror.

His magic stared back at him.

CHAUVELIN AND NIGHTSHADE got tattoos the day they were accepted into the College of the Real at Belladonna University.

Viola Vale — who was ahead of them both, charging her way up the ladder of the Department of Practical Mythology already because she was so damn smart — came along to watch, mocking them the whole time.

It was a tradition. If you were a legacy of one of the eleven families represented on the Basilisk Board (Ten Founders plus the Chauvelins, who arrived a generation later than the rest of them, but made up for it with extra wealth, power and influence) you ruled the school. You were on track to earn your status as a warlock, not merely a witch. You studied magic, and only magic. You walked into every room as if you owned the place.

Magical tattoos, infused with expensive enchantments, were

even better than clothes or cars for showing how fucking elite you thought you were.

Nightshade got a silver dragon inked across his back, spreading over both of his pointy shoulder blades. It breathed blue-green flames that licked up his neck when he was in a foul mood. When you ran your finger over its tail, the dragon hummed.

Chauvelin chose a phoenix. She covered his right shoulder, curving down over his chest. Bright gold and orange with flecks of green showing up intensely against his brown skin.

After he lost his magic, he didn't lose his phoenix. She continued to move, and dance. Her wings still fluttered; her eyes still glowed from time to time. He thought for a while that this might be a sign that his magic wasn't completely gone. His father thought so too; whenever they sat before a new high-priced healer or shadowmancer to explain the situation, one of the first things Nicolas Chauvelin would do was push his son's shirt aside to show the movement of the tattoo.

Some of the experts told his father what he wanted to hear. Others were just as bad those arseholes at his parents' parties: pity in their eyes, or a sneer on their lips.

Eventually Chauvelin did his own research. He learned that magical tattoos held the magic of the artist who had made them, not the wearer. They recharged themselves based on the magic in the air around the wearer; but you could apply one to a complete magical null and the tattoo would still move if that person held hands with a witch for long enough. You could put one on a *cat*.

These days, the wings of the phoenix flapped more slowly. Maybe because Ferd spent more time around non-magical or low magical people than he ever had in his old life. For the last couple of months, the phoenix had slept. She barely twitched, only moving first thing in the morning, after Ferd had slept with full skin contact against Hebe for several hours.

Last night, he shared a bed with Dec, both of them fully clothed, with a suitably 'bro' amount of space between them. Dec didn't had enough magic in him to cheat at cards on a good day.

But the phoenix was moving now. Not only that: she was glowing. As Ferd stared at her, she shimmied before his eyes, slowly turned a loop-the-loop and opened her beak in a silent scream.

FERD COULD HEAR someone moving around in the flat. The floorboards creaked. Sooner or later, someone would come into this bathroom and catch him staring at his chest. They'd see the shadow print on the fridge. They'd know…

What would they even know? It couldn't be *that*.

Ferd's magic wasn't coming back.

Coming to terms with his magic never coming back was one of the hardest things he'd ever done in his life. Cutting off contact with the family who kept pressuring him about it was the second hardest thing.

Ten months ago, he walked up to a help desk to change his enrolment from the College of the Real to the College of the Unreal.

That turned out to be the best day of his life. It was the day he properly met Hebe, and learned about the room for rent in the flat upstairs from her. He found new friends in Sage and Dec, two blokes with radically different magical levels who had no opinions about what he was studying, or what he wanted to do with his life.

It was the day his life started again.

And now…

Was it over? If his magic was back, was all that for nothing?

He hadn't done anything different recently. Hadn't lifted a curse or drunk a potion or taken up yoga or done any of the things the various quacks had all promised his parents would make a difference.

He hadn't undergone drastic surgery, or had his blood replaced or immersed himself in an ancient language or sacrificed a freaking goat.

All he could remember doing last night, was drinking one gulp of sangria, and kissing Jules Nightshade on the mouth.

Fuck.

He heard the floorboards creak again, in one of the bedrooms. It could be Vale, who never let him get away with anything. It could be Sage, who had more magic than the rest of them put together and would know right away if Ferd was different. It could be some rando who'd slept on the floor, about to waltz in here and wish him a Happy New Year. It could be Jules Nightshade…

Ferd left the flat, pulling his shirt on as he went. He didn't have a plan. He just needed to be away from here.

Happy Bloody New Year.

I WOKE up in my own bed, alone, which… yeah. Probably for the best. Me and Nightshade were in a weird place, and all of my other recent hookups were… well, not unsatisfying. Pointless, maybe.

Shit, was I growing up?

Hebe keeps saying stuff like 'you'd make a good boyfriend, Sage, if you only let yourself.' Swinging endorsement from the first and only girl I ever went out with. But it's a habit now. Sex and people I care about, in two very separate boxes. The only one I let get under my skin in recent months was Nightshade, and that one's so complicated it needs a whole separate box and maybe a private wiki to keep up with the nuances.

Do I want to find some lovely bloke, walk around like Hebe and Ferd with our hands in each other's pockets? Fucked if I know. But waking up on my own, the morning after a blinding New Year's Eve, that was a whole different kind of unsatisfying.

I dragged myself out to the kitchen, still off balance. Some good citizen had put the coffee on, and not drunk a drop. Weirdo. I gulped down half a cup of hot black, and breathed out as the noise in my head dulled to a quiet roar. It was a holiday. No exams, no gigs coming up. I didn't need my magic to be sharp and at the ready. I didn't need my magic at all. Sweet.

Five weeks to go and I'd be back at uni, taking Honours in

Demonstrative Thaumaturgical Phenomena. Finally, the bastards made me pick a side. It was gonna be weird, studying one discipline instead of my usual three. Apart from that, I was looking at the same old grind. Proving to the professors over and over that I'm smart enough to use the stupid big-arse power levels I've got bubbling away in here.

Three years and a triple major under my belt, and the arseholes of academia still roll their eyes behind my back about how I'm some a hick from the sticks. Like I haven't noticed they all reckon it's a crying shame that someone of my abilities was born without a basilisk sigil hanging over his silver-plated cradle. I swear, some of the Profs still think I'm faking how bloody good I am.

You wanna talk about satisfying? Satisfying was watching the crotchety old fossils fighting over who would get me as an Honours student. They don't respect me, but they don't want their colleagues to have me. In the end, the reason I chose Dem Thaum Phen over Practical Magery was because Professor Bulfinch Snodgrass from PracMag once suggested I sign up for elocution lessons before submitting a conference paper.

I get a weird feeling in my stomach whenever I think about how I've signed up for another year of uni bullshit, but whatever. I promised Auntie Sheena I'd make something of myself when she rescued me from my shithole childhood, and this is my path. I'm good at it.

The best revenge is success, right?

I was mulling that over when I turned around with my hand still wrapped around the coffee cup, and I saw it. The handprint on the fridge. And my world narrowed down, hard. That was a *shadow mark*. No wonder I was on edge. Had someone brought a freaking shadowmancer into our flat? A wildly out of control one, by the look of it.

My magic was dulled by that first gulp the early morning caffeine, so tracking the magical signature wasn't likely to be an option. But I placed my big hand over the shape of the fingers of the shadow anyway, and I *knew*. Maybe my magic recognised him, or maybe just — I'd known all along we were due for

something catastrophically shit-tastic to happen here in the
Manic Pixie Dream House. Things had been too cruisey for too
long.

I always figured if the world ever ends, it'd be on New
Year's Day. Nice and tidy.

I grabbed my phone from its overnight charger — wrapped
in cords and salt to keep it from being transformed into a frog or
a charred sooty mark every time my magic arced up against
technology. That was less of a risk right now, thanks to the
coffee.

I paused before texting Ferd. How much of a dickhead would
I look like if I was wrong? We weren't quite the kind of friends
who texted R U OK to each other, though maybe we should be.
He was probably tucked up with Hebe downstairs, happy and
content. He might be…

I looked back at the shadow shape on the fridge and I *knew* it
was his hand.

I texted: *Need me to bring you a coffee?*

See, that was good. Innocent. The sort of thing any mate
might text another after a big party.

Almost immediately Ferd texted back:

Beach. Yeah. Please. Don't tell anyone else.

Beach? We were like, an hour from the nearest beach.
Unless… fuck.

Basilisk Beach? I texted, to confirm.

Ferd replied with a thumbs up emoji. Then:

Took your broom. Sorry.

Np, I texted back. Normally I'd go off on any mate who took
my broom without asking, but this was an emergency. I'd have
to drive, anyway, with this cup of coffee in my veins (no way I
wasn't gonna drain the cup before I left the flat). *See you soon*, I
texted.

So. Shit. Ferd fucken Chauvelin had his magic back.

CHAPTER THREE

VIOLA DIDN'T BRING A JUMPER

VIOLA VALE LIKED SAGE'S room best in this ridiculous share house. Not only because there was always an esoteric magical book to rifle through, or an awesome band t-shirt to steal. There was something about Sage's room that felt comfortable to her. It was her happy place.

(If she gave it any thought, she might come up with the theory that because Sage's magic was fire-y like hers, his territory automatically felt like her territory, but she never gave it that much thought. Besides, as far as Viola was concerned, any territory she wanted was automatically her territory.)

Then there was Dec's room. She had spent most of her time there, when visiting the top floor of the Manic Pixie Dream House (stupid name) because she had been careless enough to get attached to the warm-eyed artist who lived there. His room was the opposite of comfortable — always full of half-finished sculptures and crates of stinky materials even though he had a perfectly good studio in the garage downstairs. And the little dolls for gaming, of course: they lined four shelves and were always staring down at her with their swords and axes and dragons and whatever.

Sage's room had vinyl records and half-finished homework, and no pressure. Dec's room had always been full of reminders of why they were very different people, with a blinking expiry date on their relationship.

Last night, though. Last night, she slept in Chauv's bed.

Viola had hardly spent any time here at all since Chauv moved in to the Manic Pixie Dream House. She knew what his room was supposed to look like, from the beautiful magazine-spread beach view mansion where his family lived. She remembered the colour of the curtains, the shelves of rare books, the antique cabinet of amulets. The deep dressing room she had always coveted because it was twice the size of hers. The carpet that felt like soft hugs under your bare feet.

His room here in the Dream House was very different. It had no history to it. Almost no Chauv at all; not the Chauv she had known since they were kids. He had a shelf for uni work, and another for books he was reading. A poster of the Floating Orchestra on one wall that had been left there by the previous occupant.

The wardrobe was a free standing one, clunky on three of its four legs and acquired from something called a Tip Shop, about which Viola had firmly not asked further questions.

There was a grand mirror and a bright silken bedspread, which Chauv had brought from home. But the whole place felt un-lived in. Temporary. There were no traces of the smell and feel of Ferdinand Chauvelin here, because... there was no trace of the version of him she had known for so many years, no scent of shadow magic sticking to every surface.

It was a quiet place to sleep, but it unsettled Viola. She shouldn't have agreed to stay here after the colossal fuck up that was last night's party. At least she had Nightshade with her.

Viola hated sleeping with men. Or, indeed, sleeping with anyone. How were you supposed to line up your body with a whole other person, juggling pillows and covers? She didn't like being breathed on, or being touched while asleep, or having to limit where she put her feet.

Dec had been great in bed when he was awake and paying attention — one of the many bonus features that came with the whole Dec package — but awful to sleep beside. His shoulders took up more space than they should, and he constantly turned over and over like a rotisserie chicken. How did someone with so little magic pour out so much heat at night? Viola ran warm too, so between them they created a tropical storm between midnight and morning. It was exhausting, and sweaty. (It was over now, so hardly worth dwelling upon.)

Jules Nightshade was the best boy to sleep with, despite (maybe because) he had no interest in taking off her clothes. Viola began his training at the age of seven or so, every time the two of them fell asleep in front of mirror marathons of action movies or cartoons while their parents had long dinner parties and plotted to take over the world.

Jules Nightshade stayed where he was put. His arms and legs took up less space than you might expect, and his spine was the perfect shape for Viola to lean gently against. (Her no physical contact rule was unnecessary for Nightshade, probably because her magic recognised him as so thoroughly her territory that he might as well be one of her own limbs, or a body pillow.)

Oh, and his magic was ice-cool, balancing hers out so that together they created the perfect climate control, all night long.

———

VIOLA AWOKE COLD. Was Jules dreaming of ice-flying again? It felt like Chauv's silken bedspread had transformed overnight into thick igloo bricks, weighing her down.

She wasn't even touching Jules. What the hell?

Still half asleep, she rolled into him, cuddling against his back to warm him up, but instead she felt heat scorching his side of the bed.

Viola opened her eyes, and found tiny beaded fringes of ice hanging from her eyelashes.

"What the fuck?" she groaned.

Jules, elfin and elegant in his sleep, so pretty when his sarcasm defences were not yet engaged, opened his own eyes. "Vale," he said with a yawn. "Did I freeze you? Sorry, love."

"Are you feverish?" she asked at the same time, pressing her cool — too cold — hand against his scorching forehead. "What's wrong with you?"

She saw the moment when the hangover hit him. "I think I'm going to be sick," Jules groaned, folding himself over her entire body so he could yarf over the side of the bed.

"Don't you dare," Viola ordered him, smacking his shoulder.

A horrible look went over his face, and he retched once. A glowing ball of fire vomited out of his mouth, and set the carpet alight.

CHAPTER FOUR
THIS USED TO BE FERD'S BEACH

MOST KIDS, Ferd knew, didn't grow up with a private beach a stone's throw from their house.

It wasn't technically a private beach but he knew better than to be pedantic about ownership when you had a beauty like this on your doorstep.

There was a strip of four enormous houses, at the far end of the suburb that he had once overheard a fellow student describe as 'Richy McRichTown,' which just about summed it up. Each of the houses was not only massive, but surrounded by epic gardens, a stupid luxury this close to the city. Two of the four had tennis courts. Three of the four had outdoor swimming pools, lined with artisanal mosaic tile. (The fourth, Ferd knew, had an entire underground swimming pool to make up for not having the open air one)

All four houses had high-end magical security wards, water views, and a direct path to Basilisk Beach.

While the beach was not technically private in any official sense, the nearby wards of the houses meant that if you were not one of the four families who owned this end of town, or a family guest, you would not be able to set foot on this particular sheltered stretch of sand without feeling deeply uncomfortable, like sand crabs were scratching up and down your entire body.

Ferd wasn't sure what would feel worse, as he touched down

on the sand, astride Sage's broomstick. Being rejected by the wards because he didn't belong to Number Three Bellingbroke Grove anymore, or not sensing the 'you don't belong here' wards because his magic was gone.

His magic wasn't gone. And, apparently, no one had officially revoked his family status. The sand, crunching softly under his feet, felt like home.

(He could fly again, actually *fly*, instead of being tagged along on a broomstick by a mate taking pity on him, that was something to add to his list to be happy about later, once he was done freaking out.)

Ferd had spent many hours right here, in his early teens, relishing that he had access to this place so close to home, and yet reasonably private. The houses were surrounded by leafy trees, and built up on such an angle that their water views were of the ocean itself, not the beach; you could not see anything but the furthest edge of the sand from any of the windows.

Vale and Nightshade loved hanging out here, making the most of being his friend. Nightshade had actually lived in one of the Bellingbroke Grove sea-view mansions as a kid, though after the divorce it was sold to a retired Hollywood actor; Nightshade and his mother moved into the penthouse suite of the Morgana Hotel before Ferd and his family moved here.

Vale's father Victor owned an older and darker house deeper into the same leafy suburb, laden with heavy warlock history, and lacking in beach views. Every summer, from the age of fourteen, Vale basically lived on this beach, in a series of increasingly tiny bikinis.

The three bitchy teens would hide from the sharp sunshine under massive unfolding parasol tents, eating ice creams, sneaking beers, and complaining about the world.

My beach, he thought now, feeling the sand under his feet. He abandoned his shoes and socks, and Sage's broomstick, in a pile and took off, feeling his way back into his old sanctuary. As he walked, he left dark footprints behind him; not just imprints in the sand.

Veins of darkness bled from his feet as Ferd walked towards the water. Shadows.

He knew what to do with them. Knew how to manipulate them, twist them into tools. He knew how to roll shadows thin, how to sharpen them, how to feed back on them to build his power. He had been working on these skills and techniques his whole life; the first nearly-two years at Belladonna University was a revelation of the power he could wield.

Shadowmancy was one of the most versatile and potentially dangerous forms of magic. Anything you could do magically, you could do with a shadow.

He'd done without it all last year. His world was all about making do without magic. Accepting there was nothing left. Building a new life that belonged entirely to him — not to his family or his magical heritage.

Could he do this again? Could he sink into the magic, and trust it to stay with him forever? Did he even want that?

Ferd had no idea how long he stood on the beach, agonising about it all. Eventually, he heard Sage's voice behind him. Something tightened in his stomach, then released.

He wasn't alone any more. That was a start.

"Hey, mate," said Sage gently, approaching like Ferd might be a guard dog about to bite. "So if I get a parking ticket for leaving my beat up old van in a street where only beautiful Italian sports cars and tiny Japanese hybrids are allowed, you'll spot me, right?"

Ferd laughed, a little too hard. "Sure. But around here they don't fine you money. You'll get a designer haiku on your windshield for the first warning, and a fireball hex if you do it again."

"Good to know." Sage came closer, circling around until he was within Ferd's line of sight. He held a keep cup loosely in one hand; Ferd could smell the coffee inside. Ferd knew if he looked back, he would see evidence that Sage had avoided stepping on his darkened footprints, sensibly steering clear of the shadows. Sage's power was fire and force and light; he'd have been a shit shadowmancer, but he wasn't an idiot. "How you doing, man?"

Ferd laughed again, and this one was closer to a sob. "I'll let you know."

Sage looked up and down the sweep of the beach. "I drank a cup of coffee," he said after a minute. "So I'm a bit dulled. I can't see it like I might if... but I can feel it. The shape of your magic. When did it come back?"

"Pretty much just now. This morning." Ferd's voice came out flat. Why did this feel so devastating? Why wasn't he throwing a party? (Part of him wanted to grab that keep cup off Sage and down the coffee in one gulp, to put off having to deal with this for a little longer)

He was a few hundred metres from his family home. He could go in and see them right now. They would know... they would see... and they throw a freaking party. This whole last year could be washed away in an instant, as if it had never happened. If his family was good at anything, it was ignoring uncomfortable truths. This would be a blip they never talked about.

"Want to talk about it?" asked Sage.

"Nope."

"Right."

The thing about Sage, the really great thing about Sage, was that he got it. He'd dealt with so much awful family shit in his own past, that he never assumed it was all going to be okay. He never said 'this probably isn't as bad as you think.'

Not that Hebe ever said that sort of thing, but Ferd knew she had to think it sometimes. How could she not? She came from a happy, loving family. They talked about their problems, when they had them. They supported each other, no matter what. She had no idea what it was like to be a Chauvelin. (To be loved conditionally, if at all.)

"Wanna hear a story?" Sage asked after a moment, dropping to the sand. It was still early. Gonna be a hot one, probably, but the sun hadn't started setting fire to the sand yet, and they were close to the shade of the trees. The ocean was clear blue, so sharp it hurt the eyes.

"Okay," said Ferd, after a moment. "Tell me a story."

You show me your baggage, and... I can pretend mine doesn't exist for a little longer.

CHAPTER FIVE
FROM THE JOURNAL OF THE PATIENT AND KIND MISS JUNIPER CRESSWELL, SOURCE OF HANGOVER CURES AND GENTLE THERAPY

Ms VIOLA VALE (Bachelor of Magic, Hons. First Class) has many excellent qualities. They don't always spring immediately to mind when she is in the room, but it can't be denied. She is beautiful, intelligent, and excellent at puncturing egos that require this on a regular basis for the sake of group harmony. She has nice hair. It's always shiny. She can also be incredibly kind, if she thinks she can get away with it without consequences.

For such a tiny person, she has majestic projection skills. If my mother met her, she would campaign to have her trained up as an opera singer.

When she fights, Viola is loud.

Unfortunately for the rest of us, Viola had been fighting a lot lately — with Dec, for the most part. As the residential halls were closed over summer, I'd been crashing with Holly, Hebe and Mei in the downstairs flat, usually in Hebe's room — her queen-sized bed kept transforming itself into beautifully made up twin beds, to make me feel welcome. With Dec's room right above Hebe's I had a front row seat (so to speak) to the catastrophic unfolding of his relationship with Viola over the last month or so.

It had all been rather quiet, in the week and a half since the Summer Solstice. I thought they'd broken up, or were on a break, or in suspension of relations, or some other phrase that meant they had gone to their respective corners to take some deep breaths and reassess things. But now...

I woke up to the screaming. They were clearly back together, if she was yelling at him like that. But then I realised the screaming wasn't coming from directly above me... and it didn't sound like angry Viola at all. She sounded scared, and freaked out, and...

"Hebe." I nudged my neighbour. "Something's going on."

"Ugh," Hebe muttered into her arm. "Tell Holly to pipe down until a civilised hour."

"It's not Holly." I slipped out of bed, my long nightgown un-crumpling to nearly the floor. "It's Viola."

"Can't she just break up with him and be done with it?" Hebe woke up properly then, and looked annoyed at herself. "Oh. That was mean. I'm trying to quit that."

"Come on." I didn't wait for her to decide whether she was still avoiding her own boyfriend, and hurried out of the ground floor flat to the stairs that led up, to the other flat.

They never lock the internal doors, which shows how much they all trust each other around here. The Manic Pixie Dream House has always felt more like one big share house than two separate residences.

As I stepped into the kitchen, I noticed a big black shadow mark on the fridge. Before I could investigate that fully, I saw Dec step out of his own room, into the living room beyond, wearing pyjama pants and nothing else. "V, what the —" he started to say, and a snowball hit him in the face. An actual ball of snow. He staggered back, looking startled.

I could smell smoke, dark thick smoke like someone had been burning bacon. The kitchen was clear, but when I ran into the living room, I saw...

Well.

A blackened, miserable Jules Nightshade (also without a shirt, gentlemen of today have no shame!) stood beside Viola. Her hair spiked up around her head, like a jet black dandelion. She had one arm outstretched in Dec's direction, and looked horrified. "I didn't," she said, with another frustrated wave of her arm. Three icicles, sharp and devastating, shot from her hand into the door frame beside me.

"Stop gesturing at people!" Jules howled, and what was left of his boxer shorts promptly burst into flame.

Nothing made sense. Viola's powers were the fire ones, weren't they, like Sage? And Jules was... oh.

"You've been cursed," I said quickly. "Stand very still, both of you. Try to suppress your magic. Dec? Go carefully to the kitchen, no sudden movements, and bring us two cups of coffee."

"Coffee," screeched Viola. "Why did no one think of coffee?"

It started to snow, quite gently, from the ceiling.

"Hey," said Jules, frowning. "What happened to the —"

The fire alarm went off.

CHAPTER SIX
SAGE ISN'T MUCH HELP

IF THERE'S one thing my tragic love life has going for it, it's a non-stop collection of hilarious anecdotes to dine out on.

This last month was particularly rough, with the second wave of consequences of me dating Hot Goth Barista and (completely by accident) his Equally Hot Goth Twin Brother.

It made for a funny story now, with most of the bruises healed and the emotional scars well and truly drowned.

Ferd wasn't listening to a word of my epic saga of Will and Evan. He hadn't touched the coffee yet, and the magic sparking off him was getting more intense. He smelled like a storm about to wreck the world.

The sand around him responded to his power, dancing around in patterns and whorls like it was trying to get his attention. It wouldn't shock me if the tide started shifting in his general direction because yeah. What he had bubbling under the surface was *that* big.

I broke off halfway through the story. "Mate. Want to talk about it yet?"

"Nothing to talk about," Ferd said hollowly. "Only —" he turned, looking shattered. "I don't remember anything much about last night. A few fragments."

"Makes sense." Great feats of magical energy have been known to cause reverse hangovers. You felt the effects before you did them, sometimes — and a common side effect was memory loss. That was why all Advanced Real Studies included a heavy emphasis on responsible note taking.

"I remember some things," he added. "I think."

"Any clue why this is happening now?"

"Not that," he said. "Something else."

"I know you and Hebe have been sort of weird around each other lately but you're solid, right…"

"I kissed Jules," Ferd blurted out. "Or he kissed me — I don't know. Shit. I don't know *why*."

A surge of rage overwhelmed me, blotting out the sun. Fuck. I had to hold it together. This coffee was his emergency supply, not mine. My magic was still holding quiet thanks to my first caffeine of the day, so at least my rage couldn't manifest in some kind of Ferd-eating earthquake.

No, if I let it loose, it was going to express itself by punching him in the face.

I had to hold back on that too. I'd learned my lesson when it came to Hebe. I wasn't allowed to go around playing big brother on her when it came to relationships. Over-protectiveness is dodgy in an ex, especially one who didn't come out of the relationship covered in gold stars himself. I had to play it cool for now, and let her do her own punching, if Ferd deserved it.

Maybe I should sit on my hands, to be on the safe side.

"Which is it?" I asked. "Bit of a difference there, mate, if you kissed him, or he kissed you."

A further flare of rage rolled through me. It was… entirely possible that one was all about Jules. Apparently I was possessive in all kinds of directions today. Fun new revelations.

"I don't remember," said Ferd, sounding genuinely freaked out.

"It was a party," I managed. "Bit of stray kissing, to be expected. Probably just messing around, right? Drinking game."

Nah, life was never that easy. If kissing Jules was the one thing he remembered about the night before his freaking magic came back, it was significant. It meant something.

"One thing at a time," I said, shoving that away for now. "Magic. Gotta be dealt with. Anyone you need to tell?"

That got a reaction and a half. Ferd looked horrified. "No. *Why would I tell anyone* —"

"Because you came here," I said steadily. "Mate. We could have had a deep and meaningful in our backyard, or on the train to Sydney, or a paddock halfway between here and the Dandenongs. You came home."

"This isn't home any more," Ferd said, hunching over miserably.

"Worried you might make your folks a little too happy?"

"To see me 'fixed' overnight without any sacrifice on their part? Yeah, just a bit." He shrugged. "At least I'll be able to talk to my parents again. Without them threatening to mutilate me for the slim possibility of getting their original son back. Except, after all that — I don't *want* to talk to them. I don't want them to be relieved and erase everything that happened. I don't want them to even know about this."

"Ha," I said. "You know, my parents would rather I was dead than magical. They'd sign over everything they own to trade for your situation. At least, your situation yesterday. The no magic situation."

Ferd gave me an odd look. "Were you raised in a cult?"

"Little bit. C'mon, Ferd, work with me. You came here. So either you want them to know, or your subconscious does. No way your olds won't get wind of a simmering warlock-level magic kid of their own blood hanging out on their fancy pants mansion beach. Let alone a dirtbag like me, messing up all their nice things."

The sand around us both rippled. The beach had started building a sandcastle on the other side of Ferd, all detailed with hollowed-out windows and lacy buttresses. He hadn't noticed, though its second tier of towers reached up to shoulder height.

"You're right," Ferd said abruptly, leaping to his feet. We shouldn't be here. I have to —"

There was a sound. A soft human gasp, coming from across the sand. We both spun around.

A girl stood at the edge of the beach, her face shadowed by the trees. She was about our age, and looked a hell of a lot like Ferd. Long, shiny black hair, and a miserable expression. Long brown legs, in tiny pyjama shorts and a tank top. Damn it, his family made people pretty.

"Ferdinand," she breathed.

Ferd didn't look happy to see her. His whole face went prickly. He stepped back, and his foot sank into the high end sandcastle that the beach had been building to welcome him home. "Sadie. What are you —"

"It worked!" she said, her eyes on the shadow veins that bled from his feet into the sand, flaring out like the world's slowest explosion. I could see them now, where I'd only felt the slightest whisper of them before. That's how powerful they were. "Oh, Ferdinand. They did it!"

Ferd looked beyond gutted now. He looked like someone had slammed him in the throat.

Probably for the best I hadn't punched him.

"Sadie," said Ferd in a hoarse whisper. "What the hell did they do?"

IT SHOULD BE COMFORTING that this time, the fire alarm actually went off because of unexpected fire and not for reasons involving unexpected possums in the roof, sharply plucked electric guitars, or energetic sex between two consenting magically dense humans.

No, comforting isn't the word that I would use.

Our fire alarm is an intense, sweeping magical field with shrieking sirens, and it makes you feel like your brain has been scoured with someone else's toothbrush. There's a sprinkler system, but mostly what it sprinkles is more magic.

Ugh, I need to get my own place. A tiny little bedsit somewhere with no sister, no friends, no drama, and no fire alarm.

(The last part is unrealistic, because regulations. And as for the rest of it… well. It's not realistic because I love everyone I live with, damn them all.)

I'd barely made it up the stairs before everyone else came rocketing down, and the siren hounded us out further, on to the grass out the back.

Viola was shivering. She wore one of Sage's favourite band shirts and tiny boy shorts, but mostly she was cold because it was literally snowing on her head. Snowing out of nowhere. On the first of January, right here in the city.

Jules stood off to one side, wearing only a towel someone

had thrown at him on the way out of the house. Possibly me! He stared at his hands like he'd never seen them before.

No one had given either of them coffee yet. Dec had snagged the pot on the way out but he was holding on to it grimly, no cups in sight.

"Cursed," said Juniper. "They've swapped powers. My sisters used to threaten to do this to me all the time…"

"Nope, I'm out," said Kenneth, Holly's latest bloke, fully dressed and already tapping his phone. "Later, babe."

Never mind about Kenneth. We don't care about him. Well, Holly might.

"No one invited you to stick around," Holly flung at him, turning her back.

Okay, Holly didn't care about Kenneth either.

"I don't believe this," said Viola, holding up her hand. An icicle formed on her palm, spiky and perfect. "I'm an ice troll."

"I keep setting fire to things," Jules growled. "Why would anyone ever want to set fire to things? What's it good for?"

"I find candles very calming," Juniper blurted out, and then stared at the grass. "Sorry." Her cello Irene rested again her hip. She'd darted back to our flat to get it as the siren went off, and hadn't made it out quite fast enough, so her braids were damp from the sprinklers.

I passed her an extra towel, which my magic conjured for me. The second it passed into her hands, another appeared over my shoulder.

Juniper immediately started using the towel… on her cello instead of herself. That's musicians for you.

Holly circled both Jules and Viola, fascinated. She'd taken a keen interest in magical theory recently, ever since she decided it was a lot like song writing, and coincidentally (not coincidentally) as soon as she no longer had to attend lectures on the topic. "Your magic has swapped, right? That's rare."

"It's horrendous," snapped Viola. "Of course it's rare. There have been like, twelve cases per year in Australia. Most of them due to curses, or massive feats of magic going wrong. Literal body swapping is more common." She gave Jules a suspicious look. "What did you do, Nightshade?"

"Don't look at me, darling," he yelped. "School is out forever. I've barely used my magic for more than hair straightening charms in a fortnight. And I haven't had time to offend anyone so drastically they might curse me in at least a month."

"Maybe that's it," said Mei, who was sitting cross legged on the grass with her laptop open, and a mirror glowing in front of her, searching for active cases. "I mean, sure, someone might have cursed you. I want to curse both of you most of the time. But is it possible that Jules not using his magic led to buildup of…"

"Swapping magic is a precise art," Viola said sharply. "Hardly anyone's ever actually pulled it off as a deliberate magical feat. Most of the recorded cases in the last two centuries have been accidental side effects from other curses or other great charms of power. Bonding spells mostly."

Holly leaned in, and yelped with delight as the end of her hair, still fire engine red from the Solstice celebrations, crackled with frost. "Are you two on together?"

"WHAT?" Jules and Viola said in unison, horrified.

"He's the gayest of the gay," said Viola, as if this should be obvious.

"I approve this message," Jules snapped back, his eyes narrowed as he looked at her. "Wait. Could a kiss do it?"

"Shut up," Viola said in a low, fierce growl.

This was interesting. "Have you two been kissing?" I asked, getting in only a beat ahead of my twin, who looked like she had won some kind of gossip prize.

"We have not," said Viola, obviously trying to tell Jules to shut up with her eyes. "That's not a thing we do."

Jules ignored whatever message she was sending. "Didn't Prof Thaddeon present a whole thing on failed bonding spells and their side effects for that Curse-breaking seminar series last winter, Vale?"

"You didn't turn up to any of those seminars," she said.

"I went to like, half of that one. And then I went and listened to his TED Talk afterwards because it gave me an idea for one of my final essays. Prof Thaddeon's the hot one with the goatee, right?"

Viola sighed. "No wonder you remember him. And the seminar was about accidental bonding spells, not failed bonding spells…"

Jules continued. "Yeah, yeah, usually sparked by some kind of unexpected intimacy between high powered warlocks…"

"So you have been kissing!" said Holly. She stroked her imaginary beard. "Interesting."

"Not each other," said Dec in a low voice. He hadn't spoken since we all came outside. Everyone looked at him.

I'd been worried about Dec, lately, when I had time to think about anyone other than myself. He wasn't his usual chill Dec-ness. I'd spent most of the last week and a half staying with my Mums after the Summer Solstice disaster, and he barely even replied to my texts, even the ones about live action remake of The Zombie Files which I knew he had to have a lot of opinions about.

"I will break your paintbrushes, Dec," Viola said in a chilly voice, turning on him.. "I will burn your dice, one by one. I will…" It started snowing in a circle around her, wide enough for a hula hoop. "Fuck. Jules, how do I turn that off?"

"I don't know, I haven't made it snow since I was fourteen and perfecting the art of jacking off," Jules said helpfully.

"I will break everyone's paintbrushes!" Viola screamed at the sky.

Would they even notice if I gave up and went back inside? I was tired and grumpy, and actually the fire alarm might be less stressful than this.

"If kissing caused you two to accidentally bond and swap your magic, I want to know who you've been kissing," pestered Holly.

"Kissing doesn't swap magic," Viola snapped back. "And I haven't kissed Jules other than ironically on the forehead for years."

"They both kissed Ferd," said Dec, still very calm and quiet. "At the party. Last night. If anyone's interested."

And suddenly this whole magic swap thing wasn't a vaguely interesting curiosity any more. It definitely wasn't funny, if it ever had been. "Wait," I said before I could stop myself. "What kind of kissing are we talking about?"

"The kind he should probably have told his girlfriend about," said Dec. Calmest of us all, even under these circumstances. I wanted to throw something at him.

"Viola," I said quietly. "Is he right?" It wasn't any of my business. Nothing to get upset about. I'd been at that entire party, and if I didn't want Ferd to go around kissing people, maybe I shouldn't have been avoiding him all night. (Also, a tiny voice inside reminded me, there were a whole lot of reasons why I should be more upset about the kissing Jules thing than the kissing Viola thing.)

But I'd never really considered *Jules* to be my friend. Viola Vale, on the other hand…

Viola stared at me, with an expression I'd never seen on her face before. It looked a lot like guilt. Which… I guess was better than if she didn't feel bad about it?

Another towel appeared in my arms, then another, and another. They kept stacking up, one by one, alternating in colours, perfectly folded. My magic, of course, sensed the stress in the air, and wanted to make extra sure that I was looking after everyone. Sometimes I want to kick my magic in the shins.

"Hey," said Jules Nightshade, sounding somewhat panicked. "My hand is on fire. Anyone? Anyone?"

CHAPTER EIGHT
FERD IS A HOMEWRECKER

FERD HAD NEVER MEANT Sage McClaren, of all people, to see his house.

He knew some of Sage's story. Raised in an anti-magic town in the middle of nowhere, suppressed for his whole childhood. Rescued by some aunt and brought to the city, cut off ruthlessly by every other member of his family.

That wasn't anything like Ferd's story. Ferd's story was... well, it wasn't great, but it was embarrassing to compare their situations. Sage lost everything when he was still a kid. Ferd's relationship with his parents was rough since the accident, sure. They wanted him to keep pushing to get his powers back, to do whatever it took. Ferd wanted to move on with his life.

They never actually kicked him out. They hated his choices, but they still signed the cheques. Paid his rent, so he could keep studying (subjects they disapproved of) without getting a job or four like most of his housemates.

He was the one who walked away.

Neither his mother or father had spoken to him in months, but they hadn't made him choose between his new life and the life they wanted for him, not *irrevocably*. There were probably a bunch of parenting manuals somewhere in this house, assuring them that if they gave him a hard ultimatum, it would encourage him to rebel. That kindness kept the path of communication open.

This house.

Ferd hadn't been back here in ages. Not since he moved the last of his shirts into the little room on the top floor of the Manic Pixie Dream House.

There had been a formal invitation for the Summer Solstice, hadn't there? He remembered thinking about it, even considering the possibility of introducing them to Hebe, but that had been a rocky week and in the end, he didn't have the energy to go through with it.

He had not set foot in this house in months, and something had changed since then.

It didn't feel… right.

There was a heaviness about the walls. Even the windows in this big airy open foyer felt like they were glaring at him. Like he was a stranger.

"So," said Sadie, walking ahead of them both in her tiny shorts and tank, like she'd just rolled out of bed. "Before you say anything…"

"Aren't you supposed to be in Paris?" Ferd blurted out. He didn't remember the last time he and Sadie even texted each other, or Skyped. They weren't like Holly and Hebe, as siblings went. Sadie checked in with him every week after the accident, but when he pulled away from their parents, he stopped responding to her texts as well. (Part of him just didn't want to find out if she would take his side, or theirs)

She gave him an odd sort of smile now. "I came home for the Solstice."

Oh, right. That made sense. "Sorry," he said quickly. "That I flaked on coming home, I mean. Didn't realise you'd be here."

Now she looked worried. "Ferdinand," she said softly. "We saw each other ten days ago. On the Summer Solstice. Here, in this house. Do you really not remember?"

Ferd swallowed. His fingers crackled with power. This was… he couldn't. "Sage," he said shakily. "You should go home."

You couldn't tell Sage McClaren what to do. He folded his arms, which only made his shoulders look more enormous. "Not leaving you, mate."

Sadie gave Sage a withering glare, which brought a wash of nostalgia with it. Sadie made a point of hating all of Ferd's friends. "What do you think I'm going to do to him, Mr Muscles?"

"I'm not worried about you, princess," said Sage, getting in touch with his inner arsehole, as he always did in times of stress. "I'm worried about this house. It feels fucken toxic." He turned on Ferd, eyes blazing. "I'm not imagining that, right? I'm assuming this isn't normal for you lot. It feels *cursed*."

"It's a traditional warlock house," Ferd said dismissively. "They always feel cursed. But you're right, this is…" Wrong. Different. Strange.

He bolted for the huge staircase.

"Wait!" Sadie called behind him, but he wasn't going to stop.

Ferd's magic, buzzing and fierce and not at home yet inside his skin, should be happy to be here. Chauvelin Manor, the family estate and territory. The house should be happy to have him here, especially now he was magical again.

"Where are the snakes?" he demanded as he made it to the first floor, facing off against the Mistresses, a series of famous paintings by Geneuve, a distant ancestor of whom the Chauvelins were particularly proud. "Where are the snakes?"

"What snakes?" demanded Sage, who had followed him closely. "Do your parents have pet snakes? What are their names, and do you dress them up in little outfits"

"Brass snakes," Ferd explained. "They normally hang from the walls here, when they're not sliding up and down the banisters or recording the personal data of house strangers…"

"Charming, your family," observed Sage.

"They're gone." The paintings were wrong, too. Usually when you were this close to the Mistresses, you could hear the melodic charmed soundtrack, played by a long-dead orchestra and recorded forever in oil paint. Today, nothing. Not a bell. He kept going, up to the next landing.

"Wait," Sadie complained, but she trailed behind them, not making much of an effort to hold him back.

Ferd hesitated only a moment before pushing his way into the practice studio.

This was the family hub, far more so than the kitchen or the living room or the conservatory. They didn't so much congregate here as constantly bicker over who got to use the perfect space in the house for magical activity.

It had belonged to the Tallalay family before the Chauvelins moved in: six generations of high powered warlocks who had been hanging around this neck of the woods since long before Federation. The Tallalays were shadowmancers and weather-workers, which meant wide open windows on two sides of the massive room, a skylight at the perfect angle for observing the Southern Cross, and so much power soaked into the walls that you could lean against them and get a magical contact high from decades past.

Ferd had never felt more assured, more in control, more completely himself than when he stood in this room with its bare floor and walls, its thick wax candles and century-old blackwood chests containing his own family's magical history: athames and crystals and talismans and books inherited from great-great-great-grandrelatives.

Today, it felt like a room. Just a room. Quiet. Empty. Dead. He should have felt a satisfying hum when he stepped in here, his magic back again. Not to mention, the wards on this place should have flung Sage on his arse for strolling in as a stranger to the house, without any kind of formal oath to guard their secrets. Ferd should have felt himself recharging, this close to the core. Instead, the room tugged weakly at him, begging for scraps.

"What have they done to the house?" Ferd asked Sadie in despair. "All the magic has been squeezed out of it like an orange."

"A lot's changed," she said, and now she was looking at him very strangely indeed. "Ferdinand. You must remember some of it."

"Some of what?"

She waved an exhausted arm around the empty practice studio, looking bleak. "They did this for you."

CHAPTER NINE
VIOLA IS THE WORST, PROBABLY

HERE'S THE THING: Viola didn't like people. Pretty much at all. She was distant from her family, she was constantly at war with her friends, and as for her most recent ex, well…

Yeah. She had liked Dec for longer than she usually liked anyone.

If there was such a thing as a slow burn surprise, then that was how Viola had figured out that she liked Hebe. It was a creeping, sneaky thing. But one day, she looked around and realised that Hebe was like, one of her favourite people.

Despite being so, well. Nice. And good. And *geeky*. And dating Chauv, which usually made Viola loathe just about anyone.

Hebe was pretty great. They were strong allies in the whole keep-Chauvelin-in-one-piece project. Viola genuinely never wanted to cause her pain. They were friends now, despite her best attempts to avoid that state of being.

Only, there was that thing. That happened last night. That she hadn't even admitted to herself yet. (And when that thing was happening, she hadn't thought about Hebe at all.)

"In my defence," Viola said now, glaring at Dec from across the back yard of the Manic Pixie Dream House. "There were vodka oranges. And there was sangria. And it was New Year's Eve. And Jules was being a knob."

It was Dec's fault, if it was anyone's fault. If she and Dec hadn't finally cast the final hex on their maybe-probably-yes-okay-breakup at the Summer Solstice, then Viola could have ditched most of last night's party, and spent New Year's Eve in her preferred manner, which was to say, wearing pyjamas and watching old movies and being smug about all those losers out there trying to have a good time.

But no, she had to make a point about how great she was at being single, by partying harder than she had in years. (It occurred to her halfway through the night that Dec would probably have been more jealous if she found some friends to play board games with than he would about her slinking around in a tiny dress at five different parties last night... but by then, she was in too deep.

To cap it all off, she had to get all distracted and furious and confused by Chauv and Jules' completely inappropriate behaviour in the back yard...

And...

No excuses.

"Hebe," she started to say now, but Hebe cut her off.

"It doesn't matter."

"Of course it matters —"

"Dec, stop trying to cause trouble," Hebe added, which was fair.

"But I have to —" Viola started to say, though where was she even going with this? Apologising? She hated apologising, except when it was happening to her.

"Stop," Hebe shrieked, and it wasn't about Chauv any more, if it ever had been.

Viola stared in horror at her arm, and the ice spikes jutting out of every spare inch of skin. "I hate this so much!" she declared. "Why is this happening?" (*Karma?* suggested a mean voice in her head that sounded exactly like something she would say if this was happening to someone else. *What do you think you need to be punished for, Viola? Being the worst? Fair enough, carry on.*)

"Hey," said a slightly warmer voice at her elbow, and Dec

held out the coffee pot, looking shamefaced. "I didn't bring cups," he said, which was almost but not quite an apology.

"Here," said Hebe, dropping her armful of completely unnecessary towels, which continued to be perfectly stacked even as they hit the grass. Two Fake Geek Girl mugs appeared in her hands, conjured from the draining board upstairs.

Viola accepted her mug quickly, drinking deep. The coffee was bitter and entirely lacking in vanilla syrup but it would do. The spiky ice retracted from her arm, and the unfamiliar magic subsided into a low, curdling chill inside her stomach.

Jules drank from the mug Hebe handed to him, and pulled a face to match Viola's. He liked his coffee at least twelve times more sugary than she did.

"Sorry," Dec added in a low voice to Viola. An actual apology. Wonders would never cease.

"So you should be," she said haughtily. "Talk about a dick move. This morning is random enough without…"

"I know. That's why I'm sorry."

"You broke up with me, remember," she said in a low hiss, in case he had forgotten. Mutual, the whole thing had been horribly mutual, but he said it first, so he got to be the bad guy. She wasn't sure how she felt about that.

"I remember." That sounded like an apology too.

"This is a prank!" Jules said suddenly. "Gotta be."

Viola rolled her eyes at him. "So glad you and your attention span won't be in any more of my classes. Didn't we *just say* this is an incredibly rare magical event and it almost never happens on purpose? You'd have to be a super high end mega-warlock to pull off something like this."

"Yeah," said Jules. "And I don't see Sage here. Or Chauv. Speaking of unreasonable levels of cosmic power."

Viola glanced around quickly, but of course he was right. Dec's little sideswipe would have been a lot more catastrophic if those two were here to ramp up the drama. "That could mean anything." It was a weird duo to be missing, though. "Did they even crash here last night?"

"Ferd did," Dec volunteered. "He bunked in with me."

"Sage wouldn't do this," Hebe said firmly. "It's not his style. And... obviously not Ferd."

Obviously not, because Chauvelin didn't have magic any more. Plus he knew better than to prank Viola, who prided herself on her creative streak of cruelty.

"I would totally do this, because it's hilarious," said Holly brightly, leaning over Mei, who tapped something into a mirror. "But I'm not that powerful. And I don't know how. But it's super funny, prank wise."

"Sage isn't replying on his phone," said Juniper, holding hers to her ear.

"Or on Mirrorweb," said Mei. "Hebes, have you called Ferd?"

"No," said Hebe, very quickly. "And I'm not going to. Someone else do it."

Viola gave her a searching look, then pulled out her own phone, and texted Chauvelin.

WHERE ARE YOU?

No reply. Rude.

"There's probably a few professors at the College of the Real who could help us," Viola started to say, already mentally cancelling out all the worst ones to bring a problem like this to. Professor Medeous would be smug and judgy and set them a ton of extra-curricular research before she deigned to be helpful. Professor Thaddeon? Maybe. He had presented that curse-breaking seminar, after all but everyone knew he was all theory, no practical use.

Professor Fordyce could be an option. Not only because he was the youngest and hottest new Prof in the College of the Real. He was the one who asked all the crunchy questions at the end of the seminar, challenging several of Thaddeon's premises of research, as well as his personal dress sense. Yeah. Maybe.

"Boo, no uni, we just got out of that place," scoffed Holly.

"Some of us are still there," Viola said sharply. "And what else are we going to do? Drink coffee every day and hope this goes away on its own? You're not the one flinging snow knives at your friends."

"Drinking coffee and hoping is a better plan than what I was thinking," was Holly's alarming response.

A sound cut through the morning. Viola stared at her phone. "Chauv's calling me."

"On the phone?" said Mei, sounding outraged. "Without texting first?"

Viola answered the call. Her fingers still felt clumsy, like they would spike icicles through anything she touched. She hated feeling so out of control. Magic was the thing she was best at. Being bitchy, obscure research that hardly anyone cared about, excellent magical abilities and a trust fund were all she had going for her.

"Chauv?" she said, hoping someone else would tell him that everyone knew who he was kissing last night.

"Vale," said the wrong voice.

Viola prickled with worry. "Sage, what the hell's going on?"

"We're at his place. Like, his old place. Beachfront Gothic Nightmare Avenue?"

"Shit," she said, startled. That was unexpected in so many ways. Ferd had been avoiding his home for weeks. "Why?"

"Long story, babe. Can you get here fast? And bring Hebe. We're going to need her."

"What?" yelped a faraway voice, barely audible over the phone. Chauvelin. "No, don't bring Hebe."

"Bring Hebe," Sage said with emphasis, and ended the call.

Everyone was staring at Viola. "Does anyone have a car?" she asked weakly. "Or, uh. A boatload of broomsticks?"

CHAPTER TEN
SAGE DOESN'T DO HOUSES

MAGIC USERS and their real estate. It's a whole thing. The more time you spend between certain walls, the more they soak up who you are, and how you practice magic. Everything from the paint to the carpet to the furniture becomes like a ghost of every choice you've ever made.

The Hallow Mums, their place is like that. Generations of Hallows have cast spells in that farm house, and it feels like family. It feels like them.

The Manic Pixie Dream House is newer — we've only been there a couple of years. But it's already started, that faint wash of 'us' that fills it. Give us about three more decades, and I'd recognise a teacup that once passed through our kitchen sink.

This house… should have punched me in the face with how awesome it was. That's the real dream for fancy Basilisk Board warlock families, right? A house that drips with their own magical privilege, heritage, and other things that rhyme with edge. A personal signature, bleeding under the wallpaper.

Instead, this place tasted like day-old paint at the back of my throat. Someone had stripped it bare. Recently.

Our Ferd was not taking it well, which was par for the course of how he was handling everything right now. After his sister dropped the Summer Solstice bomb, he reeled away from her and stared out the window a bunch. "I should have known," he muttered to himself. "Of course it wasn't going to just come back on its own. Of course they pulled some epic sacrificial shit just like I warned them not to, because what I want is never important."

Sadie's magic wasn't anything like her brother's. It was elegant and careful, like a cool breeze sweeping past a designer perfume factory. Finishing school magic, Vale explained once — from when some scion of an upmarket family (usually a girl) gets sent off to have her minor magic polished and prettied up, to cover the fact that her levels are as basic as they come.

Basic sons of fancy families don't have to bother with that shit, they just get poured into designer suits and given high up company jobs where they can order around people with more magic than they have in their little finger. If only Ferd's lab accident bumped him down to basic, his family could have worked with it.

But no one on the Basilisk Board wants a null in the family.

Looking at Ferd now, his stormy magic crumpled around him like a coat about to explode, I sort of saw their point. Having a kid born into their family with this level of untapped power must have been like all their Solstices came at once. Even I wanted to lick his neck.

(No wonder Jules had been crushing on his best mate for years. Bad enough Ferd looks like he should be modelling scarves or cigars in a Paris magazine shoot, but power like this? If I was Jules, I'd have thrown myself into Ferd's lap years ago, before anyone else had a chance.)

"I can't remember," Ferd said now, hands braced angrily against the window sill. "Why can't I remember? I'm sure I didn't come to the Solstice. It was Hebe's graduation day…"

"Yeah, you blew that off," I volunteered helpfully. "You never turned up. Not the ceremony, anyway. I think you came later?" It was a wild night. Art show, karaoke at the pub, secret nightclub, intense late night dungeons and dragons sesh, me dodging angry barista to hang out with Jules instead… "You definitely showed at some point, but it was late. Hebe was spitting chips."

Ferd's shoulders hunched. "I was going to go to her gradua-tion. Why wouldn't I go?"

"You were here," Sadie spoke up. "You came to the house. Maybe it was to tell Mum and Dad you wouldn't be staying for lunch? I know you had some kind of blazing row with Dad in his study. And then we all came in here…" She shrugged, looking uncomfortable. "It was set up already. I thought it was for a healing ritual."

Ferd turned around, furious. "I didn't ask for a fucking healing ritual!"

"Settle, petal," she said sharply. "I didn't do this to you."

"No, you sat back and watched while they did it."

"They didn't do anything to you either!" Sadie looked close to tears. "They did it to our house. Filled the circle with all the magic they could drain from our home. And you were so ungrateful. They gave up everything and you were going to walk away."

"Good!" Ferd yelled at her. "I *wanted* to walk away. That was my choice, Sadie. I should never have come back here."

"What happened to the magic?" I interrupted. "They didn't just — shove the house magic in Ferd. That wouldn't work, right?" I was dredging my Demonstrative Thaumaturgical Phenomena studies now. You could store a person's magic in an inanimate object for a while — and for some of the old warlocks, a while meant a century or two. But I'd never heard of it going the other way.

"They had a void crystal," said Sadie miserably. "They sacri-ficed the house's magic."

"What?" Ferd looked blank. "But that's stupid. What a waste."

"It worked, didn't it?" she flung at him.

"No. Of course it didn't *work*. My magic didn't suddenly come back because of some pointless eldritch faith ritual." He looked momentarily horrified. "This is my magic, right? It's not… the house's magic? I would know the difference."

"Don't look at me, mate," I advised him. "We didn't exactly hang out back when you were fully juiced, so I don't know what your magic is supposed to be like. But you taste like a shadow-mancer right now."

He nodded and held a hand out to the nearest wall. A black mark blossomed there like a bruise, and then was swallowed by the cream paintwork. "What they did wasn't a sacrifice, Sadie. It was vandalism. You can't go around emptying houses of centuries of magical history."

Some more details from an old Dem Thaum Phen lecture came back to me in a rush. "Uh no, you can't. You really can't. We should get out of here. This could get bad, fast."

Sadie gave me a scornful look. "I'm not leaving my house because of some superstition. We have to wait for Mum and Dad. They'll be back from brunch soon, and they'll be so pleased to see you, Ferdinand. So pleased that it…"

"Don't say it worked," Ferd barked at her. "Nothing worked. And if you think I'm waiting around so they can be all smug about this incredibly fucked up situation, then…" His expression changed suddenly. "Sage. Shit. I can't move my hand." He tugged at his palm, which was connected to the white wall of the practice studio.

I went over to him, feeling his magic burn against mine as I approached. It didn't want me near him, and neither did the house. The floor shook underfoot. Sadie cried out as she fell over. She leaped up immediately and ran to the door, but the doorknob sparked at her touch. "I can't open it!"

No time to worry about a lack of exits right now. I let my own momentum carry me to Ferd.

He couldn't free his hand, and he was burning up hot.

Black veins of magic ran from his palm into the wall.

"It's trying to feed on my magic," he said, outraged. "What the hell?"

"Yeah well, your parents starved it," I said, hovering close but making sure not to touch the walls myself. Bad enough I was making contact with the floor. Shit, the floor. Ferd's feet were still bare. "This house is hungry."

I looked down, and saw more black veins of magic running

out of Ferd's feet into the polished floorboards. Shit on a sandwich.

I took a deep breath, mentally running through the horror stories I'd heard about magic houses gone bad. Turned against their owners. Starved of magic. You don't want a magical house to go hungry, that's when shit like the Fall of Camelot goes down. Nero's Golden House. Atlantis.

We needed Vale and her Practical Mythology expertise here, like now. We needed all the Dem Thaum Phen professors on speed-dial. No. We needed Hebe. Hebe was good with houses.

I pulled out my phone, wrapped as always in cords and salt because tech and magic don't always love each other. A bolt of black lightning crashed up out of the floorboards and smashed my phone into the ceiling. Salt and bits of metal fell around us.

"Grab mine," said Ferd, breathing hard. "All the house has to work with right now is shadowmancy taken from me. It won't recognise my phone as an enemy."

Seemed like a long shot, but I wasn't arguing. I slid out his phone — in a fancy schmancy magic proofed leather case, isn't it nice to have money — and saw there were a bunch of texts, including one from Vale. I put a call through fast, and she picked up like she'd been waiting for it.

"Chauv?"

"Vale," I said calmly.

She sounded anything but calm to find me on Ferd's phone. "Sage, what the hell's going on?"

"We're at his place. Like, his old place. Beachfront Gothic Nightmare Avenue?"

"Shit," she said, startled. "Why?"

"Long story, babe. Can you get here fast? And bring Hebe. We're going to need her."

"What?" Ferd said, swinging around and gasping with pain as his arm didn't twist that way. "No, don't bring Hebe."

"Too late." I'd already hung up. "She's coming. You need house magic. Domestic shit. All I've got to throw at this problem is power and in case you hadn't noticed, your house wants to eat all available power with a spoon. Anyway, why shouldn't I call her?" Was he embarrassed to be stuck to a wall in front of his girlfriend? Cute.

"Uh," said Ferd's sister hesitantly. "Is that the same Hebe who broke up with him a week ago? Are you sure she's going to want to help us?"

I stared at her. Ferd's mouth fell open, just as shocked.

"WHAT?" we demanded in unison.

CHAPTER ELEVEN
MISS JUNIPER CRESSWELL IS NOT GOING TO MAKE THINGS AWKWARD.

DEAR DIARY,

It is not an exaggeration to say that attempting to transport the usual inhabitants of the Manic Pixie Dream House to another location in a hurry, without Hebe's usual pre-planned scheduling mojo incorporating a highly calculated system for treats and bribes, is somewhat like herding a horde of cursed cats.

Sage had taken the band van already. This left us with Mei's tiny Volkswagen as our only alternative method of transport to broomsticks.

This was a problem because Viola and Jules had just drunk coffee, so couldn't trust their magic on a broom, and were also the only people who had ever visited Ferd's old home. As they both refused to have anyone else boost them on a broomstick, they chose to travel in the car with Mei, Dec and Holly, leaving no one in the broomstick contingent of the mercy dash who knew where they were going.

In the end, Hebe and I chose the rather precarious and erratic method of following the car on a shallower flight path than is generally recommended over a city.

We got there in one piece, which is the main thing.

I was worried about Hebe. She wasn't talking much, but she was also clearly thinking a lot.

Luckily for me, there are no conversational expectations

when flying, so nothing that happened between the Manic Pixie Dream House and Ferd's frankly terrifying rich person warlock mansion counted as an awkward silence.

We arrived on the doorstep, the seven of us, somewhat in a state of déshabillé. Viola had insisted we not delay for anything, including getting dressed.

Hebe had managed to transform one of the towels into a pair of navy boxers for Jules, which was a relief to all of us, as it was terribly distracting being around someone wearing only a towel — no one needed to be constantly at risk of seeing a naked man first thing in the morning. We hadn't even had breakfast! As it was, he and Dec were both bare from the chest up which seemed most uncalled for even if it was clearly on the verge of becoming a very warm day.

I would be uncomfortable at visiting at a house of such evident wealth and privilege in my ordinary clothes under normal circumstances, but somehow arriving in a nightgown had pushed me all the way through social mortification to an odd sort of boldness on the other side. At least most of me was covered, unlike Viola in her teeny shorts and band t-shirt — or Holly, in an enormous t-shirt and leggings cut off mid-thigh.

Mei was the only one wearing clothes, which led me to believe either that she hadn't officially gone to bed last night, or that she took her time responding to the fire alarm. Her day clothes looked a lot like Holly's night clothes, so the distinction was moot.

Hebe was by far the most civilised of all of us, wearing summer satin pyjamas and matching espadrilles, her bright hair (still holding the red charm dye Holly insisted they both wear for graduation) caught up in a loose bun. It wasn't the kind of outfit anyone had ever seen Hebe wear in public, but by sheer accident she looked like she had just walked off the beach at an expensive resort.

It occurred to me that this was the first time she had ever visited the home of her boyfriend's parents, which must feel odd, regardless whether of there was some kind of dangerous situation unfolding.

As we all hovered there on the doorstep, improperly dressed and fretting whether a butler might appear if we pushed any of the buttons we could see down the side of the dark, carved wooden door, (I was fretting, it's possible they all had other things on their mind) there was a scraping sound from above us and a window went up.

"Oy, you lot!" Sage yelled down. "A little help? Ferd's house is trying to kill us."

Viola swung around to Hebe. "Give me your broom, Hallow."

"No," said Hebe in a sharp voice, and leaped back on to her broomstick, soaring up to the window.

I followed quickly, not wanting to leave her without backup. As I climbed ungracefully over the window ledge, Hebe shoved her broom at me, her attention already elsewhere. I leaned out and hovered them both down to the crowd below.

Before any of our friends could join us, the window slammed itself down with a ferocity that made me jump. The white paint on either side of the glass stretched and ebbed, sealing over the window. I stared at it, wishing I hadn't given up my broomstick so easily.

The paint stretching over the glass bulged into a face that glowered at me. I moved away very quickly, bumping into Sage's reassuringly broad chest.

Hebe stopped, staring at Ferd.

He was stuck, by the looks of it, one hand outstretched against the bare wall, black veins of magic pumping from his skin into... into the room. He strained against it, slowing the flow of magic from himself into the house.

"Stop it," said Hebe.

He didn't turn, didn't react. His eyes closed, he threw his head back and screamed with pain.

"Stop it!" Hebe shouted, her voice ringing out with all the authority of a Victorian governess in a British stageplay. "Let him go."

This time, the house obeyed. Ferd pulled his hand away from

the wall, looking at it in shock, then turned around and stared at his girlfriend. "Hebe," he breathed.

"Ferd," she said, painfully chilly.

Whatever was going to happen next between them, conversation-wise, the rest of us did not wish to be here to witness it. Given that there was not currently a door in this room, and all the windows were now sealed over, we had little hope of being allowed to withdraw gracefully.

"Did you break up with me on the Summer Solstice?" Ferd blurted out, his shoulders drooping in a manner that can only be described as heartbroken.

"Yes," said Hebe. "Was it not important enough for you to remember?"

That one confused him. He looked rather befuddled.

"I mean," said Sage helpfully. "You also failed to remember that your house is a magical vampire, mate…"

"Shut up, Sage," said Ferd and Hebe, gazing at each other.

"You made the house listen to you," Ferd said, flexing his hand as if it was painful.

"Houses get me," Hebe said. "Ferd, what's going on?"

"I'm not entirely sure. But it has something do do with my parents."

She stepped forward, her eyes locked on his. "Ferd?"

"Yeah."

"Why can I taste your magic?"

He took a step forward also. "Why did you break up with me?"

Hebe made an impatient sound, and threw herself forward.

Now there was kissing. A lot of it. They clung to each other like two shipwreck survivors.

As one, Sage and I whirled around and faced in the other direction, only to be met by a startlingly gorgeous, furious woman wearing even shorter shorts than Viola Vale. My face heated up, just a little, at her mere proximity, and I knew it was too much to hope that I wasn't blushing from nose to fingertip.

"Why am I holding a vase of tulips?" hissed the vision of beauty at Sage, clearly blaming him for this turn of events. The vase in her arms was very nice, and the tulips were striped. "Tulips aren't even in season."

"You just get used it," said Sage. "It's a Hebe thing."

The beautiful woman, whose long, flowing black hair looked like something in a conditioner commercial, peered around his shoulder to where Hebe and Ferd were still making out like they'd been apart for months. "And that?" she said, wrinkling her nose.

"You wait," Sage promised her. "Any minute now, the rest of our band is going to break into your scary monster house, and then we'll really raise some hell."

"Is that worse than what's going to happen when my parents come back from brunch?" she challenged him.

A look of concern crossed his face. "Aw, hell. Hebe, put your bloke down. We haven't rescued him yet!"

CHAPTER TWELVE
FERD'S MEMORY IS CLEARLY BROKEN (AND SO IS FERD)

FERDINAND CHAUVELIN always wanted to be a shadowmancer.

From a very young age, when he had the first inklings of the shape his magic was going to take when he grew up, he was fascinated by shadows. Not the ordinary kind, cast by solid objects when caught between a light source and a surface.

Little Ferdinand had been fascinated by the shadows inside words. Inside thoughts. Inside veins. He could see them, long before he had the skill to manipulate them. That, as it turned out, came easily.

Everything came easily to him. He was the heir of a great family, the friend of two brilliant witches with the potential to go darker, higher, until they reached that rare and elite rank of warlock. Magic was like breathing for Ferdinand, until it… wasn't.

The world without the shadows he had known his whole life was dim and lifeless. He lost a whole dimension to his physical senses. Even after he had come to terms with it, accepted his new identity as a man who could not control the building blocks of magic, he still had days where he felt the emptiness scrape at his insides. He had lost a part of himself. The best part of himself, he thought, on particularly bad days.

Manipulating shadows gave Chauvelin a powerful sense of

control over himself and the universe. Without it, he was a broomstick soaring wild and riderless in the air.

At least he had his memories. He had his history. He knew who he was, this new Ferd with new friends and a new purpose. And now...

What was he now?

Hebe was holding his hand. (Hebe had broken up with him.)

Sadie was standing in front of him. (Sadie wasn't even coming home for the Summer Solstice.)

His parents' house was trying to kill him. (He promised himself he would never set foot in this house ever again, not until something *changed*.)

Panic and darkness and shadows rose up around him now, until Ferd could not see the other side of them. He had his magic back, or something that looked and felt and tasted like his magic, but what had he lost? Why couldn't he remember what happened on the Solstice? Why couldn't he remember most of what happened last night?

He heard Hebe saying, "Ferd, what's wrong?" She sounded very far away.

Ferd felt the shadows rise up inside his body, taking charge of him. Magic burned and whirled before his retinas. He'd always been able to master his magic before, but now... now, he was just along for the ride.

He opened his mouth to cry out for help, but the shadows spun so fast and hard behind his eyes that there were no words possible.

The shadows came, and Ferd let them take him away.

CHAPTER THIRTEEN

NO CHAUVELIN IS GOING TO GET THE BETTER OF HEBE HALLOW: MAN, OR HOUSE

I SHOULDN'T HAVE KISSED him. I can't believe I did that. I haven't forgiven him yet, not at all.

Things were going so well, until the Solstice. We were on the same page, building a future together. I'd been accepted into a Grad Diploma of Magical Archiving, which meant I could stick around Belladonna U for another year while Ferd finished off his own Bachelor of the Unreal — delayed, of course, because he had to start mostly from scratch when he changed colleges after losing his magic.

We didn't need to worry about relationship milestones like living together, because we had found a comfortable balance between together and apart, on separate floors of the Magical Pixie Dream House.

We had problems, and arguments. Things weren't perfect. But we were doing fine. We'd fixed all the big issues. At least, I thought we had.

Then he flaked on me, on the Solstice. Ditched my graduation ceremony, and half the parties. When he did turn up, he wasn't acting like himself. Rude, dismissive. Some of the things he said…

I warned him to get his act together, because I wouldn't put up with being treated like that. He shrugged like I was nothing, like the entire relationship we'd been building all year was nothing.

"What are you going to do about it? Break up with me?"

I should have known, shouldn't I, that there was something more going on, that my Ferd wouldn't speak to me like that? Maybe. But at the time, in the moment, all I saw was that sneer on his face. It made me feel like ten types of idiot. Like every inner thought about how someone like him would never be interested in someone like me was right all along.

I was so angry, so hurt…

"Looks like it," I said, and walked away.

The next day, I went home with the Mums. Hung out with them quietly, making candles and baking cupcakes. I didn't tell Holly what had happened, or any of my friends. I wasn't ready to say it out loud, and besides, I was waiting. For the apology. For the explanation.

(I didn't want to be humiliated when I took him back, when I forgave him, because surely it was all some big, stupid mistake… a fight, not a real break up. I didn't want my friends, our shared friends, to hate him once everything was okay again.)

But then I came back for the New Year's party, and Ferd spent the whole time ignoring me for Jules and Viola. Every now and then, he met my eyes and smiled like normal, like nothing had happened. Other times, he looked through me like I wasn't even there.

And now…

Now, standing in Ferd's giant fancy house, I didn't know what to think.

I didn't get time to figure it out.

FERD'S FACE WENT STRANGE, like he couldn't focus. He slumped to the ground, his hand slackening in mine. The house didn't like that, or it liked it a little too much — the floor buckled under our feet, sagging like it was soggy rice paper instead of, well. Floor.

There was a crashing sound, and the door blew inwards.

Jules and Viola stood there, which explained the ice shards and smouldering flames in what remained of the door frame.

"Come on!" yelled Viola.

Sage scooped up Ferd like he was an armful of A/V gear, and headed for the exit. "Hebes, move!"

I stumbled after him. Juniper took my hand and pulled me along, which was a tiny bit comforting.

The house blurred around us, probably because I was crying. When had I started crying?

Then we were outside, on the lawn, surrounded by people I loved. Sage was conferring with Jules in an urgent voice, still holding Ferd in his arms.

Viola was interrogating Ferd's sister Sadie.

Everyone was talking, shouting, planning, and I couldn't stop crying like a soggy manga heroine with no plotline of my own.

The house shuddered behind us. I felt its pain. I'd never felt so hungry in my life.

Then Sage was in my face, picking me up off the ground. I hadn't even realised I was crumpled on the grass. I looked around for Ferd, and saw Dec and Jules bundling him into the back seat of Mei's tiny car. "Come on," Sage said, his voice sounding echoey to my ears. Was I in shock? Overly attached to a dying house? "Vale reckons there's a hot professor who can help us. Gotta get Ferd away from here."

No, that wasn't a good idea. Was it? Houses went bad when starved of magic, but starved of people? That was when they really lost the plot.

"Someone should stay here," I started to say.

"I'm staying," said Ferd's sister furiously. "You can all go to hell for all I care."

Holly wrapped one fierce arm around my waist.

"Your choices are hot professor, or home," my twin said firmly. "This house is not your problem, Hebes."

I was too foggy to argue with her.

(Hungry, the house was hungry. And so was I.)

"Hot professor," I said reluctantly. "Why stop making bad decisions now?"

"Like you're the one making decisions," said Viola impatiently. She was, I noticed, holding my broom. "Come on, you lot. Time for school."

CHAPTER FOURTEEN
VIOLA VALE UNVEILS THE SECRET STACKS

BELLADONNA U WAS a different place during the holidays. The looming buildings had an extra hint of gothic to them, even in the middle of the day, because the city's gargoyles only liked to hang out here when the noisy students were out of the way.

It was late morning on New Year's Day, and the heat was rising.

None of the cafes were open. Even the vending machines were looking abandoned. There were bound to be a few desperate postgrad students wedged into study carrels, but even the most freaked out thesis grinder was still likely to be in bed, hungover, or both.

Viola loved walking through campus when no one else was around. There was a weird kind of power to it, a smug self-righteousness mixed in with a delicious naughtiness, like she was getting away with secretly doing more work than anyone else.

Belladonna U had always felt more like home to her than her actual house. Also like her actual house, it was more fun when no one else was home.

Today felt unsettling, though, and not only because a barely-conscious Chauvelin was being dragged along by Sage and Jules, or because most of their crowd were in their pyjamas.

Viola still had the wrong magic, and her last swig of coffee was beginning to wear off. Usually she blazed into uni all warm and comfortable, her power sparking off the various magical hotspots on campus. Normally, she was in control.

Today, it took all of her considerable inner strength to prevent spontaneous snowmen from appearing on the paving stones.

Once she figured out *why* her ridiculous impulse to kiss Ferdinand Chauvelin last night had somehow switched her powers with Jules Nightshade, she was going to kill someone.

"Questions should be asked about why Viola has the private number of a certain dreamy Dem Thaum Phen prof in her phone?" teased Jules, clearly not worried enough about how high he was on the list of people Viola planned to murder with her bare hands.

"I have all their numbers," she told him. "I'm a postgrad. Who else are they going to text at three in the afternoon when they need someone to do their marking?"

"Where are we going?" Hebe asked suddenly. It was the first thing she had said since leaving the Chauvelin house. "There isn't a library this way. You said he was meeting us one of the libraries."

Viola had led them all away from the main plaza, and down the grassy slope towards a very narrow gap between the Saranac Caffastel Choral Hall, and the Unreal Humanities Admin Hub. "We're going to the Cloven."

"That's not a library," Hebe said, sounding frantic. "What even is that?"

"Sure it's a library," said Jules with a smirk. "The Bellestar Cloven Memorial Library and Secret Basilisk Archive. Every-one's heard of that, right?"

Hebe had gone pink in the face. "There is not a library on this campus that I've never heard of," she insisted. "I would have heard of it." She lunged at Sage. "If you knew about this and never told me…"

Sage shrugged. "Don't know why you think I'd know. My blood's not sparkly enough for this mob. No way they're going to share their secrets with the likes of me."

"But you're —" Hebe looked so offended, it was almost

funny. At least she had stopped moping about Chauv. "Sometimes I really hate this university," she said.

"Is now a bad time to mention that I knew about it?" broke in Holly.

Hebe turned on her twin in a rage. "What? You don't even *care* about magic studies."

Holly shrugged. "Campion used to bring me here all the time when we were dating. It has really good shadowy stacks for making out in."

"Hell yeah, it does," said Jules, and high-fived her. He almost dropped Chauv to do it.

The alley between the two buildings was narrow; Sage and Jules and Chauv had to go sideways to make it through. On the other side, the sunlight was blindingly bright again. Viola was starting to wish she had brought a sunhat and a water bottle. At least she'd thrown on sandals when she first heard the fire alarm.

Once or twice, she caught Dec looking at her like he wanted to ask if she was okay. It was important to shut that right down. She was fine. Everything was fine. She knew what she was doing.

"There is an *amphitheatre* back here!" Hebe declared, still outraged about warlock family privilege. "How did I not know for the last three years I was at a university with an amphitheatre?"

"It's not a real one, if that helps," said Jules brightly. "It's the secret entrance to the library."

"Why would that help?" Hebe said furiously.

Viola went down the wide granite steps of the amphitheatre. It was at its most piercingly bright and sunny right in the centre of the stage. "Don't tell anyone you heard the password from me," she warned them all.

Hebe made a scoffing sound.

"Hope you remember it," said Jules. "I always get stuck on the second paragraph."

Viola took a deep breath, and began to recite. "Dr Bellestar Cloven was awarded the Circe Cenotaph in 1883 for her ground-breaking work in four of the nine most significant magical fields…"

"SOME PASSWORD," said Mei, a little while later as they all headed down the secret tunnel that had opened on the hundredth word of Dr Cloven's academic bio. "Way beyond the usual 'include at least one capital letter, 1 number and 1 dancemoji.'"

"Dr Cloven wanted to make sure the generations of the future remembered her achievements," said Viola. "For some reason that was a significant issue for her, *Jules*."

"Hey, don't look at me," her friend yelped.

"Oh, it wasn't your great, great great-uncle who stole Cloven's research on lost Trojan potion ingredients, and scored the Quinzel Medal when he published it under his own name?"

"Don't bring Uncle Dippy into this, he's delicate."

"He's still alive?" said Dec, looking creeped out.

"Nah, he haunts my mother's second favourite car. He used to haunt the downstairs bathroom in our old house, and she really thought that selling up would get rid of him, but professor ghosts are the worst. They stick around because they've got so many grudges built up. And a high tolerance for boredom."

"Here we are," said Viola, regretting she had even started this topic. Giving Jules an opportunity to complain about his family ghosts was never a good idea.

Hebe made a small punched-in-the-stomach noise.

It was, to be fair, a beautiful library. One of Viola's favourite places on campus, despite the palaver it took to get in here. The hexagonal space was lined with bookshelves, spiralling out from the central atrium like petals on a flower.

The carpet, walls and leather furniture all shone in deep jewel colours: emerald on one side, ruby and sapphire on the other.

There was a spiral staircase leading down, down into the depths beneath the campus. There were at least seventeen floors of archive storage and reading chambers below them, and Viola had heard rumours there were extra floors that only tenured professors were allowed to access.

"Professor Fordyce should be around here somewhere, he said he wasn't leaving the library all day…" she said, glancing around.

A dry throat cleared.

Viola looked up, to where the professor stood on the mezzanine above them, leaning on a railing in his shirtsleeves with more bookshelves as his dusty but decorative background. (These were the notorious Snogging Stacks; the skeevier side of Basilisk privilege was the horrid suspicion that at least some of your friends might have been conceived here.)

"Professor Fordyce," Viola called out brightly. Her friends would never let her forget it if she called him Blaise in front of them. "You said I could bring you our problem?"

The professor glowered at her. He was far too attractive for his own good, not nearly advanced enough in age to make up for the kind of tall, dark and handsome qualities that had undergrads fluttering around him in packs. Luckily, he cultivated such a strong aura of crankiness that most students were content to crush on him from afar.

Viola was proud of herself for not developing even the slightest crush on Fordyce over the last semester. Luckily, his habit of dropping copious amounts of barely-paid work on her desk was annoying enough to cancel out his solid shoulders and brooding good looks.

Also, he was magically and academically brilliant, which meant he wasn't her type at all; if she had learned anything from her relationship with Dec, it was that she liked a man with talents as far from her own as possible.

(Good thing she and Chauv had never tried to… ugh, no, don't go there now.)

"You did say I could come over?" she said now, put off by the extra stormy expression on the professor's face.

"You, yes," he muttered. "I wasn't expecting a pyjama party. Or a rock band?" He looked at Holly as if he couldn't quite believe it, and then at Hebe like he'd never seen twins before.

Then back to Viola, apparently relieved there was only one of her. "What is this, Viola?"

"It's kind of an emergency," Viola said hopelessly, glad that she wasn't applying for jobs requiring his personal reference right this minute. She'd have time to make up for whatever terrible impression she was making right now.

"It's New Year's Day. What kind of emergency could possibly prevent you from being hungover like normal students?"

Jules and Sage both waved at him, and Chauv blinked vaguely between them.

The professor's scowl deepened. "What have you dragged me into, Viola?" he asked, more sharply than before. "That's the High Quill's son. What's wrong with him?"

Chauv retched once, and then vomited black blood all over the emerald carpet. Jules flinched, dropped his side, and accidentally set fire to the nearest chair.

"He broke up with my sister, so we hate him now," said Holly.

"That part's not relevant!" said Hebe, flushing red. "Also, *I* broke up with *him*."

"Sure, but I can't hate you," said Holly.

"It's complicated," said Viola, hoping desperately that she had picked the right professor. She really needed someone else to be in charge of all this right now.

"I can see that," said Professor Fordyce. "Luckily for you, I have a conference paper to procrastinate over. Why don't you douse Nightshade's half-arsed arson attempt, find shirts for the people who don't have shirts, and start at the beginning?"

CHAPTER FIFTEEN

THIS WOULD BE A VERY INCONVENIENT CRUSH FOR SAGE TO DEVELOP RIGHT NOW, SO IT'S NOT GOING TO HAPPEN, MATE.

So, the Department of Demonstrative Thaumaturgical Phenomena has six professors. This bloke's new, so he was the only one not sniffing around me last year to sign on as his post-grad student. I never made it to any of his classes, because the new prof always gets lumped with the firsties and other dull as dishwater courses until he's been here long enough to slide his own pet projects into the syllabus.

That's a long way round to say: I didn't know this fella from a bar of soap.

Yeah, I'd looked. He's hot, and when you start hearing about a hot new professor all the girls are swooning over, *you look*. But then I heard rumours that he was brilliant and an arsehole. As that adds up to completely my type, I'd sensibly kept my distance.

I'd got this far without inappropriate crushes on any of my teachers, and it would be shitty to fall at the final post.

What was the question again?

Oh, right. Ferd. Yeah, Ferd wasn't doing well.

He looked all clammy and spaced-out. Still conscious, but not totally with us. Whatever black gunk he'd expelled all over the good carpet perked him up a bit, but it wasn't looking good.

Prof Fordyce was all business, peering at Ferd and making notes. Every now and then he rapped out a book title and Hebe and Vale fell over themselves to go fetch it. Hebes was clearly in love with the library and really pissed off about it at the same time. Vale, who knew her way around this place better than the rest of us, was smug and showing off a bit.

Me? Books are a necessary evil when you work with magic. I never got on great with libraries. They hate it when you bring in snacks or play loud music, so what's the point? I'd rather haul the books I need back home and get crumbs all over them as nature intended.

"Someone's been messing with void crystals," said Prof Fordyce. "I know messing around with forbidden dark magic is par for the course at a university like this…"

"It wasn't us," said Juniper in a rush, like she was worried he might give her detention.

"Yeah, messing around with forbidden dark magic is for firstie nerds who don't get invited to the good parties," added Holly.

Ferd's eyes went completely black for a split second. He muttered something. Shadowmancy. Good thing I'd never gone near it. My college counsellor told me it was a good idea to practice control as I grew into my magic, but she wouldn't recommend me specialising in any subject that required precision. Rude, but fair. Given how Ferd ended up thanks to his shadowmancy, I'm glad I wasn't feeling rebellious when course selection day came around.

Jules made a small noise. I swung around and looked at him, just time to see his baby blues return… from black. "What?" he said, as I stared at him.

Dec was crowding Vale. "What happened to your eyes, love?"

"Nothing, I'm fine," she said, pushing him away. "Actually, not fine. Barely holding it together, given the circumstances. Back off."

"It's all three of them," said Hebe. "Whatever happened to Ferd, it's affecting all three of them."

"Makes sense," said Mei.

"Explain," said Prof Fordyce, waving a hand expectantly.

No one really wanted to.

"Viola and Jules swapped magic overnight," Hebe said finally.

"Huh," said Fordyce, his eyes gleaming with interest. He came over and peered into Jules' face, way too close. "Fascinating. A Basilisk triangle."

"That's a myth," said Jules, staring back into the professor's eyes.

"Not necessarily." Fordyce blinked, and broke eye contact, stepping away. "Has anyone here been kissing someone they shouldn't?"

I coughed, looking around. Ferd had confided in me, but did everyone else... oh, yeah. Everyone knew. So this was going to be a fun year

Jules went bright pink. "It was a party," he protested, staring at the carpet.

"I always kiss people I shouldn't," mused Holly.

"We know," sighed Juniper. "For once, they're not talking about you."

"It could be relevant."

"How could it possibly?"

"I'm cold," said Vale.

Everyone looked at her. She was standing very still. Dec hovered nearby, like he wanted to throw a jumper over her and carry her away from all this. I knew the feeling.

"Vale," said Jules.

"Really cold," she added, with a wild shudder.

Shit. Her skin was turning blue. Ice troll blue. This was more than a bit of a chill.

"Did your magic ever do that to you?" I flung at Jules.

"Sure, when I was twelve. I got over it."

"Everyone stay back," Prof Fordyce demanded. He stalked towards Vale. "Viola. Can you hear me?"

Her eyes went black, like Ferd's. "Viola isn't here."

"Damn," said the professor.

I took a step forward. Not that there was anything I could do right now... still, I didn't get a chance, because Jules tackled me first. He's light as a broomstick, so he didn't have me over, but I stumbled for a moment. He locked his arms around my waist and burst into flame.

"What the hell?" Too long since my morning coffee, and my magic was already out of sorts with all the drama. I blasted him away from me with more force than I intended. He flew over a couple of comfy armchairs and crashed on the floor. "Jules!"

Vale let out a banshee scream and threw ice at me, spears of it. I threw up a basic shield, but one of her long ice shards impaled me in the thigh. "Fuck."

Why was I the one getting it in the neck? I hadn't kissed anyone.

Prof Fordyce clapped his hands three times. Vale crumpled like an empty t-shirt. She swayed for a moment before she fell, and the professor leaped and caught her in his arms.

Ferd fell back on the carpet, also unconscious.

Holly lurched at me, looking frantic. I waved her over to check on Jules. "He's out, too," she reported a second later.

"Breathing?" I rasped.

"He's bleeding less than you, Sage. Let's talk about that."

"What did you do to them?" Hebe asked the professor. She hadn't left Ferd's side, but she kept staring at my injured leg. Fair enough. There was… a lot of blood. It was kinda spectacular.

"Knocked them out," said Prof Fordyce efficiently. "For the best. I don't need to do the same to you, do I, son?" he asked me.

Gritting my teeth, I shook my head.

"Good. Because what's going on inside these three right now is very serious. And the last thing we need is them fighting back."

"Is this really all because of some random kissing?" Holly demanded.

"If I'm right," said Prof Fordyce, looking troubled. "There was nothing random about it at all."

NEW YEAR'S EVE, TWO YEARS AGO.

VIOLA FOUND Chauvelin on the back balcony, which was a waste of his killer suit and her killer dress, but what the hell. This party was always a waste of their time.

She could feel his magic even before she stepped out the glass doors to reach him. Shadowmancers thought they were *so* subtle, but she'd been around Chauvelin since long before he learned his many layers of control. She could taste his power in her bones.

He was going to be brilliant someday. It was annoying, though at least Chauvelin put some effort into his first year of uni studies; not like Jules who breezed in late, skipped half his lectures and somehow still did amazingly.

Her friends were the worst.

"How's your party bingo card going?" Chauv asked as Viola approached. She tugged her hem down a bit and sat carefully beside him on the cold, sculpted bench. They were in darkness here; the party areas were all carefully lit with paper lanterns, the boundaries marked out by impeccably dressed staff holding trays. This was not a party zone.

"Three inappropriate jokes said to me by men old enough to be my father, four inappropriate jokes said by my father to girls my age while I was in earshot, and three members of the Board who don't remember my name but definitely know that I'm very *young* to be going into the postgrad programme."

"Well they have known you since you were in pigtails."

"Ugh," said Viola. "I never wore pigtails. That was Jules." She eyed him. "How's your bingo card going?"

Chauv shrugged. "Professor Hekate's leaning on me to drop Dr Charmsnare's class next semester so I can work on Special Projects with her instead."

"You're the one who wanted mentorship from a Grey Ops legend. If you want to excel in the field…"

"I guess. It means my course load will be like, 75% shadowmancy."

"Oh and you were so looking forward to padding out your degree with a course in Victorian poetry," Viola said sarcastically.

Chauv laughed. "Yeah, yeah. Dad says it's good to specialise, but he also wants me to keep on with Charmsnare's class for political reasons."

Viola rolled her eyes. "No one can say our fucked up families didn't prepare us for life in academia. Everything has been for political reasons since we were picking out birthday party themes." She nudged his shoulder. "So what are you going to do?"

"Oh, both," said Chauv, like it wasn't even a question. "I don't need a life, or a girlfriend, or parties. I can just work forever, and be the perfect Basilisk son." He sounded bitter, which wasn't like him.

Viola laid her head on his shoulder. "We're literally at a party right now, and you hate it," she reminded him. She could feel the vibrations through the floor of the balcony; the music, and all the mingling magics.

"This isn't a party. This is my father and your father and their friends reminding us all how much control they have over our futures. The future warlocks of Australia. Aren't we fine?"

"You're drunk," she accused.

"Also accurate." He didn't sound drunk at all.

Viola lifted her head and made him turn to face her. His dark eyes were clear. "Chauv," she said lightly. "Are you all right?"

His mouth turned up in a soft smile, and for one terrified moment she thought he might be about to kiss her.

(That would ruin everything.)

(Wouldn't it?)

"Heyyy losers." Jules Nightshade lurched through the glass doors holding a bottle of champagne and two empty glasses. He put a glass in each of their hands, poured messy froth into both, and then dropped to the ground with his back against the railings, keeping the bottle for himself. "So this where the party is."

"Chauv can't attend parties anymore, he's too much of a swot," said Viola lazily, licking champagne off her hand thanks to Nightshade's dodgy pouring skills.

"You can talk, Ms 'submitted three formal publications before postgrad even begins' Vale," teased Chauv. The tension between them was gone, thanks to Jules. Had it ever been there?

Everything made more sense when it was the three of them together.

"Oh, so you will find time for us little people while rewriting the building blocks of magic?" Viola teased back.

"Soooo remember when I said Merryweather was super into me?" Jules broke in, sounding smug.

Viola looked closer. His hair was a mess, and his clothes had definitely been put back on in a hurry. "Oh no, she groaned. "Not *Campion*, he's such a dick."

"Hey, I could have meant his brother. You know, the nice one."

"You never choose nice over hot."

"You admit he's hot."

Chauv looked pained. "Tell me you didn't have sex in my bed. Again."

Nightshade smirked, and necked more of his champagne. "A gentleman doesn't tell."

"A gentleman definitely tells his friend if sheets need to be cleaned."

"True, true. So, I totally had sex in your bed…"

NEW YEAR'S EVE, ONE YEAR AGO

Viola was wearing a sharp dress and sharper eyebrows, but there was no one at this party to appreciate how great she looked. (No one she wanted to appreciate her, anyway, considering that most of her father's friends were like a hundred years old.)

Oh, there were plenty of sons of her father's friends hanging around in their fancy suits, but she'd pretty much blown through the best dateable and bangable options among them already. (At least, those who were dateable and/or bangable and had not already fallen into bed with Jules, which limited her options *a lot*. She tried to avoid crossover where possible.)

Anyway, it was less than inspiring to flirt with boys she had known since she was a small child. No, Viola was committed to a new plan for this year. If she bothered with men at all, she would move outside the Basilisk pool. Outside Belladonna U altogether, unless some attractive foreign postgrad caught her eye. She was tutoring firsties this year, and that meant hooking up with undergrads at the College of the Real had a whole new level of risk to it, even if most of them were the same age she was.

Speaking of problematic, she spotted Nightshade schmoozing with a handsome Bulgarian warlock who was way too old for him, and dragged him away with an apologetic smile Viola found was useful for most situations. "Where is he?" she hissed.

"I don't know, hiding from his overcompensating parents?"

No one had expected the Chauvelins to host the New Year's Party this year. Sure, it was a tradition that the High Quill of the Basilisk Board took on hosting duties, but… well. Surely Nicolas and Mereen would not want to make a spectacle of their damaged son, not with him so recently out of hospital.

Turned out, yes. They were more than happy to make a spectacle. The Chauvelins dressed in their usual glam finery, and welcomed all their peers to yet another outrageously stylish New Year's Party, as if absolutely nothing had changed.

Chauv had gone along with it at first, dressed up to the nines in a designer suit, the perfect Basilisk son. He shook hands or kissed cheeks with anyone who approached. He even smiled once or twice, when the conversation suggested that was the only appropriate response.

It was killing him.

It was breaking her heart.

Because what Chauvelin hadn't done was shake Night-shade's hand, or kiss Viola's cheek. He was avoiding them, still. He'd been weird around them ever since he came home from hospital — not returning calls, not answering texts.

She missed him so much she thought her magic was going to punch a fireball out of her chest. (And wouldn't that be diplomatic?)

"He's fine," grumbled Jules. "He's just being an arsehole because we still have *our* magic."

Viola slapped him on the arm. "You can't say that."

"Sorry, are we lying to him as well? Pretty sure he gets enough of that from Mr and Mrs Denial. Now if you'll excuse me, I have a Bulgarian to seduce."

———

VIOLA FOUND CHAUV EVENTUALLY. It was so strange having to search, not simply reach out to recognise his magic with her own. He wasn't on the balcony she thought of as theirs. It was worse than that. He was in the middle of the room, making small talk. Of course this was the one party he decided to attend properly.

She made polite but impatient niceties, hovering on the edge of the group who were all watching him carefully like he was an exhibit in a zoo. Viola caught at least two of them gently testing his magical boundaries. Without moving an inch, she stung their fingers with a soundless charm.

The crowd dispersed pretty quickly after that.

"What do you want?" Chauv growled.

"I want you to stop acting like me and Nightshade are like the rest of them," said Viola. "We're not strangers you have to playact with."

"Dance with me," Chauv said impulsively, going from distant and defensive to way too close so quickly it made her head spin. He put his hand on her waist, moving further into her space. "Come on. Let's have some fun."

"I might if you meant it," Viola said irritably. Still, dancing had to be better than being ignored, didn't it?

Chauv pressed up against her. His head tilted down, like he was angling for a kiss. "Do you want to go up to my room?" he purred, his meaning obvious.

Viola stepped back. She didn't like the intense look in his eyes. "What the hell are you doing?"

"Why not?" he demanded of her. "Why shouldn't we? Unless you're ashamed to be with me now I'm not the shadow-mancy student of the year with the big bright future."

It's not like Viola had never thought about it, her and Chauv. Hard to think of anything else when their parents had been mentally planning their wedding since they were kids. But she couldn't get past how much it would devastate Nightshade. And now — maybe he was testing her, to see how weirded out she was about him losing his magic. But proving a point was a shitty reason to sleep with someone. "I want my friend back," she told him.

His eyes flashed. "I have other offers, you know. "

"I'm so proud."

"I've collected more numbers than Nightshade tonight. You'd be amazed how many of the most powerful warlocks in this room have wives who have always wanted to fuck a null." And now she couldn't see the anger or the arrogance in him, just the hurt.

"Don't call yourself that," Viola said automatically. It was a horrible word, something kids yelled at other kids who were slower to find their magic. And the technical, exact meaning of the word, well. That was worse.

"It's what I am," he said.

"Your mother said they were looking into options," Viola said desperately. "Cures."

That, of course, was exactly the wrong thing to say.

It was months before he spoke to her again, and by then… well. By then, he had Hebe and his new accepting friends. He didn't need her at all.

———

NEW YEAR'S EVE, LAST NIGHT

So, this party sucked. Pretending to be amazingly happy so no one would guess she was miserable about the whole Dec thing was wearing Viola down to the bone. She was a bit drunk (she couldn't taste anything but sour sangria on her tongue) and she had no energy left to feel anything but hollow when she glanced out the kitchen window and saw them. Her boys. Nightshade and Chauvelin. The gay one and the straight one, both completely off limits to her and to each other.

That was how their friendship worked.

They all kept pretending that Jules' crush on Chauv had gone away when they were about fifteen, that Chauv hadn't propositioned Viola a year ago, and that nothing would ever, ever change between the three of them now they had clawed their friendship back. It was an important pretence. It was *structural*.

It was an hour before midnight on New Year's Eve when Viola looked out the kitchen window to see those two shadowy figures leaning into each other.

This is it, she thought desperately. *This is the the thing that breaks us.*

She didn't think about Hebe until later.

———

VIOLA MET them on the stairs, because apparently she couldn't even quietly flounce out of the party without being confronted with them both, Nightshade and Chauvelin, walking far too close together.

They didn't even look guilty. Chauv was dazed and glassy-eyed — was he drunk? Jules looked confused and irritable. Viola cleared her throat and gave them her most unimpressed expression.

And there was the guilt.

"Vale," Chauv started to say.

She waved him off. "I don't care. Why would I care that you're trying to wreck everything?"

"It was just a kiss," said Jules sullenly. He already sounded heart-broken which was exactly what shouldn't be happening right now. Didn't Chauv realise how easily they could lose him? How easily they could all lose each other?

They were adults now. Adults didn't have to stay friends because their parents encouraged it.

"Is this what you want?" Viola demanded of Chauv. He was clearly the one to blame here. Jules had been hiding feelings for years: of course he was going to snog back if the boy he'd always loved came at him in a darkened corner on New Year's Eve. "Because if you're going to screw up this entire friendship, it should be for both of us."

It made sense in her head. Less sense when she threw herself at Chauv, who caught her rather than letting her hurtle down the stairs because he was a gentlemen.

Viola kissed him hard. For a moment he kissed her back, his mouth open under hers. Apparently no one was making good decisions tonight.

Viola only stopped kissing Chauv when she heard a broken, wheezing sound and realised that Jules was laughing himself sick, one hand clutching the banister.

"You're the worst," he sputtered in delight rather than jealousy.

"I hate you so much," Viola flung back at him. But she was also on the edge of laughter, the kind of manic laughter that was really hard to breathe through.

"Please don't kiss me," gasped Jules. "I can't deal with

straight panic right now, it might kill me." He held his hand out, though, and she clutched him back, and they were okay.

After a moment, when she recovered herself, Viola looked at Chauv. He had made no move to get away from her painfully inappropriate advances. He looked distant, like he wasn't even there with them. He wasn't laughing.

"Are you all right?" she asked him, because someone had to.

"I have to go," Chauv said abruptly and pushed her at Jules, then headed back up to the heaving party.

"Tell me I'm an idiot," said Jules, and he wasn't laughing anymore either. He put his head in his hands and groaned.

Viola sighed, and sat next to him on the stairs. "You're such an idiot," she told him. "But everything's going to be okay. Eventually. In about a thousand years, when we're all dead."

CHAPTER SEVENTEEN

FERDINAND CHAUVELIN IS NOT AT HOME

HIS MAGIC WAS GONE. Ferd knew it was gone before he opened his eyes.

Null. A cruel, technical term. No one said it in front of him for the first month after the accident. But he knew they were thinking it — he noticed every time there was a pause, every time the word was ever so carefully *not* said in his presence.

And the worst part? It was his fault. All of it. You could blame the university. You could blame the heavy course load, the pressure placed on him by the professor in charge. You could always (an easy out) blame the parents.

When it first sank in to Ferd (the first time around) that his magic was gone, he braced himself to defend Professor Hekate and her methods. His father was High Quill of the Basilisk Board, so unlikely to bring any of his influence to bear on the university itself. But firing the professor in charge, finding someone to scapegoat, would be just like him. Ferd was ready for that.

He prepared a speech for when his father ramped up the blame game. A simple, firm, humble speech making it absolutely clear that it had been Ferd's choice to push the experiments with his magic harder and faster. His choice to go days without eating and sleeping, as he neared the results he was hoping for. All, 100% entirely his fault.

He never had to deliver the lecture, as it turned out. Weeks, months passed and no one even slightly threatened Professor Hekate's job. Finally, it sank in that his father had always known exactly who to blame.

———

FERD'S EYES SNAPPED OPEN. "VALE."

"She's fine," said a low voice, almost as familiar as Ferd's own. "You know she always needs extra beauty sleep." Jules Nightshade moved into view, looking drawn and miserable. There was a pressure that Ferd realised after a moment was Nightshade's hand squeezing his.

"What happened?" Ferd asked.

No one answered him.

They were sitting on the lush carpeted floor of the Cloven library, propped up by chairs. Ferd lifted his fuzzy head to look around, and saw a cluster of their friends nearby, all under-dressed for uni.

"Casual Friday?" he croaked.

"The man of the hour," said an unfamiliar voice.

A man with dark eyes and a sculpted five o'clock shadow — hopefully a useful professor, and not just some random — leaned in, peering at Ferd. "Your magic is gone," the bloke informed him. So yes, a professor, or possibly an over-qualified librarian.

"Obviously," said Ferd, trying for sarcasm. It came out miserable. "It wasn't even mine," he added, because he wasn't entirely stupid.

"Not this time around," agreed the probably-professor. He moved back out of Ferd's field of vision, and that was when Ferd saw it: a void crystal, twice the size of any he'd ever seen in a private home, hovering in mid-air. Dark shapes swirled inside it. Ferd knew shadow magic when he saw it.

Mine, something inside him whispered, but that was the craving of an addict, not reality.

"Did that come out of me?" he asked.

"Of all three of you," said the professor steadily. "You weren't quite yourselves, for a while there."

Ferd clutched at Jules. "Did they take yours too?" he gasped.

"Steady," said Jules in a soft voice. He held up a hand, formed a perfect spiral of snowflakes, fanning out across his palm. "All's well that ends well."

Ferd was overcome by a choking sob. If his friends had lost their magic too, and it was his fault...

"Hey," said Jules, and gave him a brisk hug, something they rarely did. "Settle, petal."

Ferd clung to him for a moment. He hated the feeling of being weak, but he could really do with a hug right now. "Words of small syllables," he said finally. "I'm not as smart as I used to be."

"Lying," sighed Jules.

Ferd looked around for Viola. It wasn't enough to be told she was all right, especially if she wasn't here at his side. Asleep? His eyes moved over the group of people he had bizarrely come to think of as family over the last year or so. Hebe and Holly curled up together in chairs, both looking unreadable with their bright, identical hair that didn't make them look remotely like they were the same person. Juniper hovered behind them. Mei was reading something on her hand mirror.

Sage sprawled, half-sitting-up on the floor with blood soaking one leg of his shorts and splattered up the front of his Fake Geek Girl t-shirt. No visible wounds. He gave a half-wave.

Dec leaned against Sage, wearing pyjama pants and a t-shirt that looked like it had been conjured out of thin air — to Ferd's eye, unadulterated by a magic field of his own, it looked like someone had lightly coloured Dec's chest in with a greylead pencil.

Viola lay, eyes closed, with her head in Dec's lap. She was very still.

"She has her magic, right?" Ferd asked anxiously. He couldn't feel it.

Dec gave him a steady shrug because, yeah, they were in the same boat. Equally fucking helpless. Ferd had never really thought about it before now, that Viola had been dating someone else without magic, for half a year or so. So unlike her.

"She does," said Jules. "I can feel it, Chauv, it's okay. Whatever Professor Guyliner here did with the void crystal switched our magics back, and uh —" he indicated the void crystal with its tumbling, swirling shadows. "There's none of me in there."

"It's the house magic," Hebe said quietly. Ferd looked back at her, startled. It wasn't like he had forgotten she was here, he just… wasn't expecting them to be on speaking terms. He had a lot of holes in his memory between the Summer Solstice and now, but he was pretty sure everything he wasn't remembering added up to a whole truckload of terrible boyfriend behaviour.

Ex-boyfriend, he remembered with a wince. Fuck.

"Professor Fordyce was going to explain," said Juniper, speaking up and then blushing wildly when everyone looked at her. She held up a notebook. "I'm taking minutes."

"Glad to know someone's organised," said Jules. Still practically draped over Ferd, but he'd better not try to move away any time soon. Jules was all that was keeping Ferd in one piece. Why wasn't Viola awake yet?

"You said this was a Basilisk Triangle," Hebe went on. "I assume that's some kind of — fancy magic that only certain privileged members of the university get to learn about? Like this library?" Of course, they were in the Cloven. Ferd had spent most of first year hanging out here, trying to impress Professor Hekate with how advanced he was. How dedicated. How special. He'd have been better off going to concerts and getting off his face every weekend like the other firsties.

"It's an ancient ritual," said Professor Fordyce. "If Ms Vale was awake, she could share her notes from Practical Mythology."

"I'm awake," muttered Viola, sounding crankier than the rest of them put together, but no crankier than usual. "I'm fine." Her eyes, slow to catch up with the rest of her, fluttered open.

Dec laid a hand on her shoulder. "Maybe don't sit up yet?" he suggested mildly.

Viola being Viola, she sat up immediately and glared at

everyone for daring to think she might need a minute to recover. "Basilisk Triangles," she declared. "A ridiculously over-powered and out-dated bonding spell. They were called Medea Triangles for centuries, though the most famous example was…"

"Oh, I know that one!" said Holly, unexpectedly. "Morgan Le Fey and her sisters. Don't look at me like that," she added to her twin when Hebe did not try to hide her surprise. "Pegasus did an amazing song about Morgan Le Fey, we were going to cover it at our next gig."

"The spell was resurrected and popularised by Isadora Tallalay, one of the Founders of the Basilisk Board here at Belladonna University," Professor Fordyce went on.

Viola sagged back a bit against Dec, still doing her best to look like she was completely fine. It took everything Ferd had not to crowd her, to demand more information. He only had Nightshade's word for it that her magic was back to normal.

The professor continued: "She used it to bond her magic to that of her close friends, Bellestar Cloven and Saranac Caffastel. It gave them a vast resource of shared magic to tap into — allowing them to exchange, borrow and amplify each other's power."

Sage coughed. "Didn't Isadora Tallalay disappear on campus during a basic resurrection lecture, like a hundred years ago? And Saranac Caffastel's the one who blew himself up with…"

"It's a very unstable spell," said Fordyce, unsmiling. "But it became popular for a while, before it was finally forbidden in the College of the Real. Still, the original spell would have been kept among the archives of the Tallalay family, as well as here at the University. We're never allowed to destroy information about magic, even when it might be in the world's best interest…"

Ferd cleared his throat, feeling sick. "The Tallalay family owned our house before we moved to Australia," he admitted.

Professor Fordyce met his gaze. "I'm aware," he said, with a slight hint of sympathy in his tone. "I actually studied the rise and fall of Isadora Tallalay for my doctorate. I thought it was a terribly clever way to get a foothold into teaching here at the infamous Belladonna U. She was a legend."

"What aren't you telling us?" asked Jules. Ferd could feel the tense line of his body beside him, vibrating with tension. "I thought you peeled this triangle spell off us. So we're okay, right? I feel normal." They both turned to look at Viola, who flipped her middle finger and then set fire to it, to prove her point.

"I hope so," sighed Fordyce. "The Basilisk Triangle is one of the most powerful and intricate of all warlock bonding spells. But it is supposed to be cast voluntarily. I am assuming that none of you consented to this particular spell? I can see why Mr Chauvelin's family may have believed it was a viable option to return some measure of his magic in combination with those of Ms Vale, and Mr Nightshade. I can even see how sacrificing the magic of their house, to substitute for his contribution, may have worked in theory. But the idea of imposing a bond like this entirely from the outside is ludicrous. Failure was inevitable, unless at least one of you participated in the casting."

Ferd felt cold all over. Slowly, he turned to look at Jules.

His friend gave him a filthy look. "Don't you dare," he said firmly. "Don't you fucking dare suspect us, Chauvelin. Vale and I knew how you felt about all those shitty attempts to fix you…"

"But if you thought it was for the best," Ferd whispered.

"It wasn't for the best," snarled Jules. "We're not idiots. You think Vale would have gone into something like a deeply problematic historical bonding spell without crosschecking oh, ten million footnotes first? *She'd still be doing the research.*"

Relief, slowly, flooded over Ferd. He knew that. He did know that. "I'm sorry," he breathed.

"You're a dick," Jules told him, which was news to exactly no one in this room. "We're not the ones who have been acting out of character, moping around being all pissy and weird and kissing people they shouldn't, and…" he paused, glancing back at the professor. "Wait, you mentioned the kissing before. Is that relevant?"

"Ah, students," said Professor Fordyce with a patronising smile. "It's amazing you get any work done. I believe from our current pool of information —" he waved his hand around the group. "This particular Basilisk Triangle spell was established at the Summer Solstice. It would have had some effect on the focal subject, Mr Chauvelin — erratic behaviour, dark impulses, patches of memory loss. Definitely best not mixed with alcohol. But to be fully triggered over the three of you… kissing is one of the ritual traditions, yes. How long before any of you felt magical repercussions?"

"After the kissing?" Jules asked.

"Yes, Mr Nightshade. After the kissing."

"Not sure. A few hours. The next morning." Jules looked at Ferd, who nodded reluctantly.

"The next morning," he agreed. Which was of course, this morning. Though this morning felt like it had lasted a year already.

"There you are, then." The professor looked smug at having figured it all out. It made Ferd want to thump him.

"Would it have worked?" he blurted out.

Fordyce blinked. "Would what have worked?"

"The Basilisk Triangle. If it hadn't… if the house hadn't gone mental on us, if Jules and Viola's powers hadn't swapped like that. Was there any chance it could have actually worked?"

"Under controlled circumstances," mused the professor. "With full consent and knowledge from all three parties — four, really, including the house — I would say the chances of the Basilisk Triangle holding steadily and giving all three of you equal access to magic are somewhere between 4 and 15 percent."

Ferd felt numb all over. Those were not good odds. "How likely was it to kill us?"

"All three of you were very lucky," Professor Fordyce said in a low voice.

Ferd swallowed hard. "My parents didn't just sacrifice their house's magic," he said. "They were willing to sacrifice Night-shade and Vale. That's so far beyond not okay."

"They might not be the only ones," said a soft voice. He turned around, and stared at Hebe. She stared back at him, not looking nearly as sympathetic as everyone else right now. "The professor said it's unlikely anyone would attempt to cast that spell without some form of consent," she said, her mouth a thin line. "You're the one who can't remember what you did on the Summer Solstice. Are you absolutely certain you weren't in on this?"

A part of him had been hoping she would forgive him for everything that had happened over the last few weeks. But no, apparently not. "You really think me capable of that?" he demanded.

Jules coughed sharply into his hand, reminding Ferd that he had been the one thinking similar accusations, only a few minutes ago.

Everyone looked shattered.

Juniper stopped writing in her notebook.

"What is the meaning of this?" boomed a voice that was usually only heard in formal university ceremonies, and occasionally at very fancy cocktail parties.

Professor Archibald Charmsnare the Seventh, Vice-Chancellor of the College of the Real, marched into the library as if he owned the place, with a crowd of familiar adults at his back. Board members, every single one of them.

Gulliver Locksley and his great-uncle Hadrian. Sorrell Merryweather. Norris Asteria. Victor Vale. Irene Nightshade with her father Julius — and, making an astonishingly rare appearance, her ex-husband West. And, of course, to top it all off, a furious-looking Nicolas and Mereen Chauvelin.

More than half the active Board (a quorum, Ferd thought, with the part of his brain that was always cynical about his father's choices… though, apparently, not cynical enough).

"I see we've found the thieves," said Ferd's father, with his usual brand of obnoxious confidence.

Shock crept over Ferd like he was having an out of body experience. *Oh*, he realised, as the Board members converged on Professor Fordyce and the void crystal. *We're fucked.*

CHAPTER EIGHTEEN
WILD CARD IS NOT HEBE'S
BRAND

"Now now," said Charmsnare. "We're dealing with students, Chauvelin. I'm sure there is an explanation for these shenanigans other than outright theft."

Under normal circumstances, I would probably be quite upset to be meeting one of Belladonna U's Vice-Chancellors under these circumstances. I'm a nerd, okay. I like to be at my best around teachers, and that wasn't going to change just because I'd recently graduated.

(Professor Charmsnare wasn't even Vice-Chancellor of the part of the university that I had graduated from. And I still would have wanted him to think Hebe bloody Hallow was smart and a follower of rules and much more responsible than her twin sister.)

Under normal circumstances, I might have had many anxious thoughts about the appearance of so many members of the legendary Basilisk Board, including *Ferd's parents*, currently looming over Professor Fordyce and threatening to have him sacked.

It was even possible that, under normal circumstances, I might be freaking out that Sage was splattered with blood (thank goodness Mei found a good Mirrorsite for healing charms, none of us are caught up on our Real First Aid certificates), *or* that

Ferd had apparently been making out with both of his best friends, *or* that I had the worst headache right now.

None of that mattered. Nothing mattered but the dark, roiling shapes of angry magic that spun wildly inside the library void crystal.

I couldn't even be angry about the existence of this secret library any more, and I thought I would be angry about that forever.

Right now, it was all about the magic.

That was all that the Chauvelin house could think about, anyway. And this was a problem for me, because the Chauvelin house had climbed inside my head, and refused to let go.

Mine, it murmured now, from deep inside my consciousness. *My magic, mine.*

Yours, I agreed.

MOST PEOPLE THINK that domestic magic was funny. I guess it is. Funny, awkward, silly, and sexist as hell. My magic manifests as magazine-perfect hints and tricks of how to be a good house-wife. Carpets literally clean themselves where I walk. Windows become cleaner when I breathe on them. (I'm an awesome flat-mate, I pull my weight and everyone else's weight just by turning up.)

And of course, there are those endless cups of tea and throw cushions that have become a running joke in my life.

Unfamiliar houses, though, especially houses with a deep magical history to them, that can be a problem. I check myself before crossing most thresholds. If a magical family has a bad history with the Hallows (we're a very old traditional witching family ourselves, don't you know) then it's best not to even go in. You never know what kinds of traps might be waiting for you.

I hadn't had time to think about it with Ferd's house earlier, because it was already on the attack. So busy worrying about my stupid boyfriend, I never gave myself a chance to put up my usual, totes necessary walls.

The Chauvelin house, once the Tallalay house, and before that not been a house at all, but a piece of land stolen and colonised and built upon… well, it didn't give a damn about my family.

But it liked me. Of course it did. The house was starving, and hurting. It was betrayed and stripped bare by its people. And there was Hebe Freaking hallow, all juicy and pink with the kind of magic most houses craved. House magic.

It climbed inside my head, and I didn't even notice, not until I stood in this library and watched Professor Fordyce drag the stolen magic physically out of my unconscious, stupid, *stupid* boyfriend. Ex-boyfriend. Whatever.

The house woke up, and licked its lips.

Mine.

"It's very clear what must be done," said the terrifying Nicolas Chauvelin of the forbidding eyebrows. "That magic —" he pointed to the void crystal, "—was removed without permission from our home. I don't know what kind of illegal experiments you are endorsing here."

"That magic," snapped Fordyce, squaring off against a whole group of people who had likely already fired him in their heads, "was removed *with permission* from your son. Who shouldn't have been carrying it in the first place."

I ignored them all, my eyes on the void crystal. It was old, and not the best quality. All it needed was a little encouragement, and it could crack. Slowly, I watched a hairline form on its surface.

"WHAT ARE YOU ACCUSING ME OF?" roared the High Quill of the Basilisk Board. Dick.

"I can't prove that you broke dozens of ethics guidelines in what you did to this young man and his friends," said Fordyce. "But if you try to blame me for your incompetent flailing, I will make sure the entire world of Real Academia knows what happened here today."

"Viola, come away," ordered a furious looking man who must be Viola's father. "You shouldn't be mixed up in this."

Viola, on her feet now and standing very close to Dec and Sage, gave him a look of utter dislike. "I didn't choose to be part of this. Do you have any idea what happens to witches or warlocks who are dragged into half-baked Basilisk Triangles without consent? Your precious High Quill was willing to risk your daughter for half a chance of getting his son's magic back."

"You don't know what you're talking about," Mr Vale said dismissively.

"I can knock you up a quick research paper if it would help," Viola shot back.

The void crystal broke. Just a sliver of a break; a long jagged fracture, but it was enough.

Mine.

"No!" cried Nicolas Chauvelin. "Stop that!"

"This is your fault!" Ferd raged in a burst, the first thing he had said to his father since the untimely interruption. Good for him, standing up to them, finally. *Too late.* "You did this to me. To all of us!"

"Everyone shut up!" yelled Professor Fordyce, already reaching for the void crystal, trying to heal the breach.

I hit him with an armchair. It rose up behind him soundlessly, and slammed him to the floor.

Everyone was looking at the void crystal, except Sage who turned and stared directly at me the second the chair hit the professor. "Hebes," he said in a broken voice. "What —"

The void crystal shattered into pieces and the dark roils of magic surged out of them, desperately flailing.

Mine, crooned the house.

Yours, I agreed.

I held out my arms, and let the magic come to me. And then, I took it home.

CHAPTER NINETEEN
SAGE IS NOT GOING TO SAVE THE DAY

OKAY, so this colossal fuckup of a day officially went nuclear when Hebe hit the hot professor with a chair. Typical Hebe move, that one. No one else would use an armchair as a weapon. There were books the weight of dumbbells within easy reach. Also, magic.

I'd been too wrapped up in all the drama, and the blood loss, to pay attention to her. I was going to regret that. Maybe forever.

Hebe was gone.

There was a second there when I was so amped up, I couldn't think what to do, how to react, other than TRAGIC LIBRARY FIRE WIPES OUT BASILISK BOARD. Let the bastards burn.

Then Holly had my arm, and she screamed something at me. I went with her. Arguing with Holly Hallow is only worth doing when you have time on your hands.

She dragged me with her, up into the stacks. I followed even though this clearly wasn't the way out. We ended up in a dead end full of heavy leather spines, and the smell of stale magic.

"Stupid rich person library with stupid rich person toys," Holly said, pulling on all the books wildly.

She'd been here before, I remembered, with her shittiest of ex-boyfriends, Campion fucken Merryweather.

One of the books twanged, and the wall slid aside to reveal…

Stupid rich person toys, oh yes. It was an armoury of wands and staffs and brooms; protection against the rabble for when revolution eventually hits this university and we all start eating warlocks instead of putting up with their privileged bullshit.

Give me a broom and a plan, and I'm a happy bloke.

We didn't have a plan yet. But that didn't stop me and Hol seizing the prettiest broomsticks from the display, and flying back out of the library like our lives depended on it.

Hebe needed us.

———

THE CHAUVELIN HOUSE WAS A WRECKED, sucking vortex of starvation and misery when we left it. This… wasn't better.

Clearly, it had its magic back, and that meant Hebe was here, somewhere. But we couldn't see her.

What we could see was the house, blazing with power. It looked like someone had decorated it for Halloween, and the theme was *these shadows are going to kill everyone you love.*

Ever seen a building glow with darkness in the middle of the hottest day of the year? It was like staring into the sun, but in reverse.

"She's in there!" Holly yelled at me.

I knew that too. Not because I had a mystical twin connection with Hebe — I didn't even believe that Holly had that, not really. But I knew a shitty situation when I saw one. Hebe brought the shadow magic back to the Chauvelin house. Hebe was nowhere in sight. There was nothing to be gained from kidding ourselves she was having a nice walk on the beach right now.

"I'm going in to get her," snarled Holly, making for the front door.

I lunged for her, grabbing her around the waist, but she was already too close for the house's comfort. A crackling flicker of darkness thrashed out at us, stinging Holly on the foot.

"Fuck!" she screamed, and we both hit the ground, me breaking her fall.

Ow. So yeah. My leg wasn't 100% unstabbed, despite Mei's best attempts at Real First Aid.

"That house has learned a lesson," I said. "It is not going to let anyone with unfamiliar magic over that threshold."

Holly turned her agonised face up to me. "But Hebe…"

"*I know*."

Hebe was overflowing with unfamiliar magic. Hebe was packed to the gills with Hallow family recipes and weaponised throw pillows. Hebe was not safe in that bloody house.

"What the hell do we do, Sage?" asked Holly.

"Wait for us to get here, obviously," answered a breathless voice. Juniper threw herself off a broomstick and ran over, with Nightshade close behind her.

"Stay back," I warned. If the house didn't want Holly near it, Jules Nightshade was going to be a mighty red flag with a cherry on top.

He gave me a scornful look. "I've been coming to this house since I was ten. I used to live next door. I have my name written under all of your tables!" he added in a loud voice, addressing the house. "Also, that chipped skirting board on the second floor? Totally caused by my attempts to look cool on a skateboard."

The shadow house rumbled, and left us all alive.

"We need Ferd," said Holly. "Now."

Jules looked up at the house, his mask of humour slipping away. "Not sure the house is going to trust him any more than it trusts us."

"But he doesn't have magic," Holly insisted.

"Do you think the house knows he's not the one who stole the magic he was carrying around earlier today?"

Holly hugged herself, miserable. "We have to get Hebe out of there."

Jules started to say something and then stopped. I met his eyes, and he gazed back at me. We'd both taken the course on Advanced Battle and Defence Magics. Once a person has been possessed by magic that properly belongs to a place, or and object... they don't always make it back in one piece. There might not be a Hebe left to come out of that house.

"What?" Holly demanded, apparently choosing now to stop being oblivious to the feelings of others. "Why the hell does your face look like that, Sage?"

"Rude."

Mei's tiny car screeched into the shady avenue. She didn't so much park as stop suddenly in the middle of the cul de sac. Everyone tumbled out: Viola and Ferd looking equally rough, Dec, Mei and — to my surprise, at least, Professor Fordyce. Dishevelled, bit bruised, still intact. Still on our side, despite Hebe's best efforts with that chair.

"Hello," the professor said cheerfully. "Yes, I probably am fired and yes, I have called the authorities and no, it's probably not a concussion. Let's see what we can do before we get interrupted, shall we?"

The authorities. That meant the cops, probably, and the paranormals, definitely. So we had a ticking clock until squad cars rolled up to agree with the Basilisk Board that we were a gang of rogue students causing trouble. Good one, prof.

"The magic isn't letting us in," Holly said frantically. "And Hebe hasn't come out!"

Ferd shook Viola off his arm and started forward, despite Nightshade yelling out to him to stop. He made it as far as the doorstep, and then the house lashed out hard, slapping him with a tendril of shadow that hit like a sonic boom. He was flung backwards, crashing into Mei's car... which gave way like a four poster bed. Professor Fordyce, at least, was shit hot on reflexive defence skills.

"Brilliant," said Nightshade, when he found his voice. "Chauv, you *moron*. This isn't your house any more."

I had an idea. And it was stupid, maybe, but I couldn't just loaf around here when Hebe might be lying somewhere in a maniacally magical house, being drained or fed on or... I don't know, punished for the terrible choices of the Chauvelin family. "Can you remove my magic?"

"What?" said the professor, sounding alarmed.

"Like, is there anything that could just… get rid of it?"

"Yes," he said slowly. "A triple shot espresso."

I was such an idiot. Why hadn't I thought of that? I whipped around. "Who has coffee?"

"No one," said Holly. "No one has coffee!"

"Literally all these houses will have coffee in them!" said Mei, waving at the street. "Start knocking on doors and looking innocent."

"How about we all keep our magic where it can be useful, shall we?" said the prof in a careful voice like we were all kindergarteners.

"Sage," said Juniper in a worried voice. "Where's Dec?"

Dec. Dec didn't have magic! Dec… had clearly figured this out, way ahead of the rest of us.

"Where the hell is he?" I asked, turning to the house. Had he gone around the back to find a way in?

The sound of breaking glass tore through the heat of the day.

Breaking things. I should have thought of that.

CHAPTER TWENTY
WE'RE ALL IN THIS TOGETHER

HEBE

THERE ARE UNHAPPY HOUSES, and then there's this.

I had all of it, for a few moments there. Every broken plate and fingerprint on the banisters. Every memory of the families who lived here, stuffed into my head like an over-ambitious mattress.

I saw a sulky Ferd and his sulkier older sister moving into this place with their elegant, impossibly beautiful parents, bringing generations of sinister warlock magic into a house already aching with sinister warlock magic.

I saw generations of the Tallalay family: brilliant, brutal, tragic. I mourned their losses and witnessed their miracles.

I breathed in the smell of the wood frame and first nails, of the mortar and cement that formed the foundations of this beautiful, terrible, miserable house.

I even held the memories of the vacant lot, all parched grass and chalk marks as the developers walked up and down in their stiff wool suits and top hats, too hot for Australian weather, making decisions about who would own what.

This house had a history and for a moment there, I held it all in my head. Then the house took it back, all of it, dragging the darkness and the sparks and the memories out of my flesh. It didn't care how much damage it did along the way. I'm lucky to still be conscious.

Mine.

I think maybe it thought my house magic could heal it, and when it became obvious that wasn't going to happen… well, it dragged the stolen magic back out of my head and left me for dead. Here. Inside a house that's either dying or about to explode shadow magic all over the city.

There are shadows everywhere. I tried leaving, but the house doesn't want to let me go. Right now, I'm hiding in the storage space under the stairs which is twelve kinds of stupid, because it's not like you can hide from a house *while inside that specific house*. It's letting me believe I can hide, and that's somehow worse.

The instability of it all is shaking me apart, from my teeth to my fingernails. This isn't going to last. The house is drunk on its own magic, but once something is broken you can't just snap your fingers and make it better. The cracks will always show. The tension points remain, waiting to snap when you finally get comfortable again…

I'm pretty sure no one will ever be able to safely live in this house.

I'm pretty sure I'm not getting out of this house alive.

And yes, all this is probably a metaphor for something. I'm sure Holly will write an amazeballs song about this someday. Hope I live to complain about it.

I can feel him coming; walking through the house. The calm presence of a person-shaped lack of magic feels like a headache charm that finally kicked in on the third try. He's coming to rescue me. *Ferd.*

It's embarrassing how glad I am about that.

But then the door swings open and I can see his wide shoulders there framed by fierce purple flame and dazzling deep shadows.

It's not Ferd, after all.

VIOLA

Viola had better things to do than prevent Chauvelin from trying to run into the house over and over, like a cartoon character who didn't know he was licked. She left Sage and Jules standing sentinel over Chauv, and went to Professor Fordyce, the only one around here who knew what he was doing.

Chauv's family home vibrated with magic and fury. Viola saw a glimpse of dark flames in the upper windows, sparking wildly. The outer shell of the house shuddered. Layers of white paint flaked off every surface. It stank of shadows, and misery, and sulphur.

"It smells wrong," Viola said in a low voice so only the professor could hear her. "Sour."

"Dead house walking," Fordyce said in a measured tone. "No saving it. The only question is how to mitigate the damage. How's your Dem Thaum Phen?"

Ugh, Demonstrative Thaumaturgical Phenomena. If they were all still undergrads, maybe they could claim extra credit for this horrendous New Year's Disaster. "Sage," Viola called out. "Prof Fordyce needs your big strong muscles."

Sage hurried over, standing on Fordyce's other side. "Got a piano needs shifting?"

"We need to set up a protective perimeter for when the house goes critical," said the professor. "Got anyone fluent in runes?"

Not if the house goes critical, Viola noted. *When*.

"Holly and Mei are handy at runes," said Sage, flexing his hands. "Is this perimeter of yours gonna stop Dec and Hebe from getting the hell out of there?"

Fordyce hesitated, only for a moment. "There's some prep work to be done," he said. "We can throw it up the second they're clear."

Sage growled under his breath. "And if they don't get clear on their own?"

"Hope that they do."

"That's not a solution, Prof."

"I know. But sending more pyjama-clad twenty-somethings into that house right now is the worst idea in a day full of truly terrible ideas."

"Mei, Holly," Viola called. "The professor needs some runework. What about me," she added. "How can I help?"

"Keep that lot away from us," said Fordyce with a wave of his hand. "We have work to do."

Viola turned, and felt a wave of sickening dread as she saw the cars drawing up near them, one after the other.

The Basilisk Board had arrived.

HEBE

"So, this has to be the stupidest thing you've ever done," I say conversationally.

Three seconds after Dec strode into the house like a big damned hero to save the day with his entire lack of magic, the house decided we weren't amusing any more. The flames got hotter, the shadows wrapped around us like a thick fog, and an invisible force shoved us back into this tiny triangular storage space and shut the door.

The house saw Dec as Not a Threat right up to the point that he tried to rescue me. So here we are, trapped together.

"I don't suppose you brought dice and paper?" I murmur, leaning back against his shoulder as he puts his arm around me. "Could get boring."

"I mean," he says, casual as anything. Even impending death from a vengeful magical house doesn't phase Dec. "I brought my phone."

Huh.

JUNIPER

I feel it vital to inform all future readers of my diary that at this point in the chaos of magical house meltdown, parents and Board members arriving, unlicensed magical practice and oh, the first police car…

I was still wearing my nightgown.

Which honestly made it feel more like a surreal dream than otherwise.

The professor had given Holly something to do, which was a relief because she was about two minutes away from a meltdown to rival that of the Chauvelin house.

Viola was trying to hold off the grown ups with her superior tone of voice and sharply plucked eyebrows.

My phone rang.

I answered it, half in shock. "Dec?"

"Juniper," said Hebe's voice. Warm, familiar, alive. "Get me Sage. I have a plan."

"SAGE!" It came out of me in a scream, which was for the best. I might otherwise have spent ten minutes trying to cough politely at him.

Sage came to me instantly, ignoring the professor. I held the phone out to him, shaking. "It's Hebe."

He leaned into the phone but didn't touch it. Even so, it sparked against his magic, practically fizzing. I held it closer to his ear, careful not to make contact with him. "Babe," he said once, and then listened. "Got it. Love you. NIGHTSHADE, VALE," he yelled, already running towards the house — no, not quite towards the house. Towards a sandy path along one side of the house. "WITH ME! Gonna blow some shit up."

Viola and Jules ran after him without hesitation. That left the Basilisk Board between us and the police car, which seemed like a great deal of misinformation waiting to happen. Another car rolled into the avenue, this one with the green stripe along the side which meant paranormal squad.

My phone was dead. I made for Ferd, who looked shaken

and miserable, standing on his own. "I can't help," he said as I approached. "I can't do anything."

"Someone needs to tell the paranormals what your parents did to you," I said in a low voice. "And make sure they don't interfere Professor Fordyce while he's trying to protect everyone."

His eyes widened. "Juniper. I can't."

"It's okay." I tucked my arm into his. I'd stand between him and the police if I had to. In my nightgown. "We'll do it together."

HEBE

I'm glad I'm here with Dec. Calm is what's needed. Calm and steady and reliable. He's a good bloke. A solid person to have at your back while you wait for your ex and your friends to blast an escape tunnel through a house that's trying to eat you alive.

We used to hook up for a while, last year… the year before last, I suppose, since it's New Year's Day. I'd never thought I was the sort of person who could be casual about anything, but it was a refreshing window of good sex and friendship that never really… went in a particular direction.

Somehow Dec became one of the people I trust most in the world, after Sage and Holly and Mei.

I thought Ferd was that, too. Someone I could trust with my entire self. Maybe he is. Maybe I was horribly unfair. He's been messed around so badly by his parents. I don't know what the hell was happening to him on the day of the Summer Solstice, but it was clearly more important (and damaging) than the graduation ceremony he missed; the parties he skipped out on; all those unanswered text messages I sent while trying not to sound like a clingy girlfriend.

It's hard not to sympathise with him now I know exactly what he grew up with.

I want to go home. Not just to the Manic Pixie Dream House. I spent a week and a half around the Mums recently, making jam in the mountains and doing nothing and… I couldn't live there forever, but it was so nice to have a break. To breathe. To be a witch instead of student—three jobs—girlfriend—unpaid band manager.

The flames are getting hotter. Like this is a house fire situation and not a… shadow magic about to explode and take out the city block situation. Both of those would be bad.

I hope I can hear Sage when he blows a way out for us. The plan will only work if I can.

"Are you and Viola really over?" I ask, for the sake of talking about something other than our current doom.

"I reckon," says Dec. "Too much drama. She needs someone who will fight with her, and that's not a good look on me."

"Makes sense." I can smell smoke, choking my throat, but it's not the kind of smoke that comes from a fire. My head hurts. If I wasn't leaning against Dec, I think I'd have hit the ground already. His hand is steady on mine. Reliable. "I don't want to be a student any more," I blurt out.

"Yeah? But you had that whole, thing you signed up for."

"Magical Archivist Diploma. It's a good course, really hard to get into. I'd probably get a job in any library in the country with one of those, from Belladonna U."

"So why don't you —"

"The Department of the Real. All those magic snobs. Hidden buildings, and Basilisk Kings, and oh those *horrible people*." The Board, all arrayed against us while we were lying around a library we weren't supposed to know about, bloodstained and miserable. "I think I'm done," I confess. "We graduated. What's the point of sticking around?"

My first day at Belladonna University, I knew I wanted to stay there forever.

"Ready for real life, then?" says Dec. A question, not a statement.

Somewhere, I hear a shout and something shaking the house.

A boom so intense that I can feel it on the back of my eyelids. I guess that's the signal.

I take a deep breath, which tastes of a hundred different kinds of magic burning all at once. My head swims, but I'm on my feet, hand on the latch of the door to the storage space. "Ready or not."

CHAPTER TWENTY-ONE
BASILISK OR NO BASILISK

FERDINAND CHAUVELIN DIDN'T SAVE Hebe.

———

THE HOUSE WAS GONE. Ferd felt it die.

When it happened, he wasn't running to the rescue of the woman he loved (that was Sage and Jules and Viola, who caused a distraction by blowing up the swimming pool at the back, long enough for Hebe and Dec to get the hell out).

He wasn't working on a magical perimeter to protect the neighbourhood (and possibly the entire city) from being damaged when the house finally gave up and imploded in a rush of damaged shadow magic. That was Mei and Holly and Professor Fordyce.

No, Ferd busy was arguing with his parents and sister, in front of the police and paranormal squad, hoping not to get arrested.

When the house died, he felt it like a mosquito sting on the back of his neck, a tiny flare of what magic used to feel like; a last gasp of shadowmancy.

It flattened everyone else. Several of the paranormals. Most of the Basilisk Board. Sadie. Juniper. Professor Fordyce. They all hit the ground when the shadows of the house gave their final wail.

Holly and Mei were still on their feet, clinging to each other as they held the runes tight to keep the house from blasting out of the locked zone.

Without his magic, Ferd saw what any magical null might see: a house dissolving into a black cloud that whirled and fought, but could not escape the runic field. For one horrible moment, he didn't know if Hebe was still in there.

Juniper's phone began to ring.

She sat up, rumpled and dizzy. Handed her phone to Ferd, like he deserved to know first. He put it to his ear. "Yeah?"

"Got 'em," said Sage. His throat was hoarse, like he'd been smoking non-stop for a week.

Ferd felt his knees shake. He couldn't stand up much longer. He caught Holly's frantic look. "They're okay."

She burst into tears.

THE REST of New Year's Day was spent in a series of beige rooms, explaining things to a series of unfriendly looking authorities. Mysteriously, most of the Basilisk Board managed to avoid this particular stage in proceedings, though that turned out to be helpful, because it meant Nicolas and Mereen Chauvelin were left with few allies to back them up.

Irene Nightshade, one of the few members of the Board who did follow to the police station, made it very clear that she intended to press charges against the Chauvelins for endangering her son. Victor Vale, who turned up about an hour after he should have done, reluctantly agreed to do the same on behalf of Viola.

Sadie cried a lot.

Viola didn't cry at all.

It was all kind of a blur.

Ferd didn't say much, well aware that he was a brown-skinned man in an Australian police station, and his parents' lawyers were unlikely to be looking out for his best interests. He couldn't rely on the family money to be safe. He couldn't rely on anyone for anything, except his friends.

At one point, Juniper sat next to him with her hand on his arm and asked a lot of earnest questions of the nearest police sergeant about family restraining orders. Later, he would probably be grateful for that.

It was all…

Hours of talking and not talking. Ferd didn't feel like he was even inside his body by the time it was all over.

———

BUT THEN THEY WERE *HOME*. Some of them changed from pyjamas into entirely different pyjamas. Pizza was ordered.

Home was the top floor of the Manic Pixie Dream House. That had been true for a long time.

At one point, Ferd staggered out to the sweltering kitchen to get a glass of water, and found himself staring at the black shadowed hand-print on the fridge for like, twenty minutes.

He only stopped when Hebe joined him in the kitchen and tucked herself up against his chest like she belonged there. They leaned companionably against the sink for a few minutes, being numb and quiet together.

He patted her hair and said, "Does this mean…"

"It's New Year's Day," she mumbled into his chest. "New beginnings."

"But does that mean…"

"Don't overthink it."

He kissed the side of her head. "You're the one who overthinks things. I'm just here to look pretty."

"No thinking," she muttered. "Not until tomorrow."

The pizza arrived. Since they were the nearest, he and Hebe trooped down the stairs to fetch it. When they returned to the living room, they tried to avoid all the meaningful looks from their friends.

Sage stuck out a leg to fake-trip Hebe, and she kicked him.

He hooked her knee and brought her down next to him for a hug. "Hey, since when do you have ink?" he teased. "I thought you were our token wholesome member of society."

"What are you talking about?" Hebe asked, baffled.

Ferd could see it too, the familiar line of a magical tattoo flickering back and forth along her collarbone, barely visible beneath the collar of the stripy pyjama top she wore. A jolt of recognition went through him, and he yanked his t-shirt off over his head.

"Dinner and a show!" hooted Viola, but then she stopped and stared at his chest with a very different expression. "Oh."

"Yeah," said Ferd. "That."

His tattoo was gone. His skin was a sea of unmarked brown from shoulder to stomach, like he had never been marked.

Sage reached for Hebe and she slapped his hand away, undoing two buttons of her pyjama shirt herself, blushing as she pushed her bare shoulder out on display.

The familiar wings of Ferd's beloved phoenix tattoo moved with surprising vigour, across Hebe's shoulder and collar-bone. There were more gold details than he remembered, and the linework was a little more delicate. It was clearly his tattoo.

"Whoa," said Jules.

Everyone was staring.

Hebe quickly buttoned herself back up again. "And that's enough of a cabaret," she said firmly.

"Are we talking about this?" Holly said, sounding a little shrill. "Because I am not cut out to be the *boring* sister."

"We're not talking about it," said Hebe, and shoved pizza in her mouth.

Over the evening, she kept glancing at Ferd, her hand moving to the place on her skin where the phoenix tattoo had chosen to live.

At some point, they were going to have to have a conversation. But not today.

———

THERE WAS a bit of clean-up required, after last night's party. Everyone moved around each other quietly, getting it done. Finally, the whole gathering collapsed into a *Bromancers* marathon, as was often the way for this lot.

Ferd slipped away for a moment to himself in the backyard. Viola located him within minutes.

"Here you are," she accused, like his escape was an insult.

Ferd leaned against the brick wall and said nothing.

Viola flounced over to sit next to him. Jules, unusually quiet, dropped to his other side.

"It doesn't have to be awkward," Viola said after a while.

Jules snorted.

"Why would it?" said Ferd sarcastically. "Just because our parents hate each other now, and mine were prepared to let you die for a slim chance of getting my magic back, and there are lawyers involved…"

"I was referring to the kissing," said Viola.

Ferd choked out a laugh. "Pretty sure we planned *never* to talk about that."

"Suits me," muttered Jules.

"So stupid," Viola sighed after a long silence that was not unawkward. "As if we need some ancient triangle spell to tell us that the three of us will always have each other's backs." Her small hand slid into Ferd's, and squeezed.

"I just thought of something," said Jules. "I'm the only one of the three of us who doesn't have to roll back up to Belladonna U in March. I'm free!"

"I hate you so much," said Viola.

"I'm going to drop out of uni and get a job as a broom weaver," said Ferd.

"Nope," said Viola. "You need a diploma for that these days." She laid her head on his shoulder. "You know how some people believe that what you do on New Year's represents how your whole year will turn out?"

"Ha," said Ferd. "That's depressing."

"No, I think it's good! This year is going to be about figuring out who we are as adults. Not defined by our parents."

"Destroying our childhood homes and betraying our child-hoods?" Ferd suggested.

"Metaphorically!" said Viola. "Well, not entirely metaphorically."

"I'm going to be devastatingly successful without losing access to my trust fund, thanks very much," said Jules.

Viola sighed. "*This* is why people find it hard to like us, Nightshade."

Jules shrugged. "Why would I need other people? I have you two."

"They're not so bad," said Ferd. "Other people."

"True," Viola said in a tone that suggested she didn't really agree with him at all. "As long as you still like us best."

There was a time in his life when people looking at Ferd and not seeing a Basilisk King seemed like the worst thing in the world. But now? It was weirdly freeing to have lost it.

"I'm going to need a new tattoo," he said, and closed his eyes while his two best friends started bickering about what design he should choose, as if they got a vote.

Sleep. He needed sleep. And tomorrow, he could start the new year all over again, as a man without magic.

The comforting sound of Viola and Jules arguing about something that was none of their business reminded him, at least, that he hadn't lost everything.

He had one more year as a student of Belladonna University, in the College of the Unreal, to figure out what came next.

A lot could happen in a year.

THE END.

THE END

ACKNOWLEDGEMENTS

This book was made possible by all my Patreon subscribers, who support me every month. Words cannot describe how grateful I am to you all, and how much my writing owes to you.

Special thanks to those who pledged high to get the very first paperback editions of *Holiday Brew*:

Ju L, Kate W, Katharine S, Adelaide P, Anna H, Koa W, Ilta A, Debbie L, Mark W, Leah C, Scott L, Jean S, Virginia S, Sidsel P, Mikayla M, Selina L, Sarah D, Ursula S, Aurora C-H, Amy R.

ALSO BY TANSY RAYNER ROBERTS

Unreal Alchemy

Power & Majesty

The Shattered City

Reign of Beasts

Cabaret of Monsters

Musketeer Space

Joyeux

Castle Charming

Merry Happy Valkyrie

Tea & Sympathetic Magic

The Frost Fair Affair

Love and Romanpunk

Please Look After This Angel & other winged stories

The Mocklore Omnibus [Splashdance Silver & Liquid Gold]

Ink Black Magic

Bounty

NON-FICTION & ESSAYS

It's Raining Musketeers

Pratchett's Women

AS EDITOR

Mother of Invention (with Rivqa Rafael)

Cranky Ladies of History (with Tehani Croft)

ABOUT THE AUTHOR

Tansy Rayner Roberts is an award-winning science fiction and fantasy author, who also writes murder mysteries as Livia Day. She lives in Tasmania with her family.

You can listen to Tansy on the Sheep Might Fly podcast, reading aloud her stories as audio serials.

Find TansyRR

Website: tansyrr.com/

Newsletter: tinyurl.com/tansyrr/

Patreon: www.patreon.com/tansyrr/

TANSY RAYNER ROBERTS

UNREAL ALCHEMY

BELLADONNA U, BOOK #1

CPSIA information can be obtained
at www.ICGtesting.com
Printed in the USA
LVHW030256210920
666626LV00019B/1493

9 780648 763925